CW01021629

To Rome With Love

To Rome With Love

D.P. Rosano

Published 2017 by Creativia (www.creativia.org)
Cover art by Cover Mint

"Rome is the city of echoes, the city of illusions,
and the city of yearning."
- Giotto di Bondone, Italian painter and architect

Dinner with Julie

March 2017

My fork plied the leaves of bright green lettuce on the plate. It shuffled the crisp half-moons of red pepper and toasted slivers of almond while it flicked bits of sesame seed and toppled droplets of the dressing from each layer to the one below.

I say my fork did all this because it seemed to be detached from me, held by a hand that mindlessly stirred the assembled salad without any motive force from my brain.

"Mom?" Julie's voice seemed to appear suddenly from a void, although she was sitting next to me at the kitchen table. Her question drew me from my thoughts.

"You seem so quiet," she added. "Everything okay?"

"Of course, honey. Of course." To prove my point, I stabbed some lettuce and plunged it into my mouth. Julie continued staring at me, showing a bit of concern and I wanted to reassure her.

But how could I reassure her without telling her the whole story.

"Your father loved you very much, Julie." That opening sounded odd even to me. What did my daughter's father who passed away two years ago have to do with my blue state this evening?

"And, of course, I did," I added. "I mean, I do, of course!" An embarrassed chuckle caught in my throat at my sudden inability to speak clearly.

My hand resumed stirring the contents of the salad plate while my gaze wandered over the carved pattern of the chairback across from me, teasing out every curl and rosette etched into the darkened wood frame of the chair.

My eyes were searching mindlessly in much the same way that my hand was stirring carelessly through the salad.

"Giorgio."

I spoke the name out without much thought or hesitation, then wondered whether my tongue had taken a cue from my disconnected hand and eyes.

"Huh?" Julie asked.

I engaged my brain just in time, realized that I was on the doorstep of a story that Julie had never heard, a story that would bring some pain, one that might fill in gaps in my history that she didn't even know existed. But my toes were on the threshold, and I felt that now, suddenly, I couldn't pull them back out of the doorway.

"Giorgio," I repeated, and I began to tell my dear daughter of the man before her father.

Piazza della Repubblica, Rome

March 1985

Tammy's head was tilted back to allow the warm rays of afternoon sun light her face. She was sitting on the stone wall around the fountain in Piazza della Repubblica, her hand resting beside her hip as she closed her eyes and opened her other senses to the city sounds and smells that swept over her.

The rub-rub of bicycle tires mingled with the occasional car horn and light screech of tires from the Fiats and Alfa Romeos careening around the circular traffic pattern of the piazza. Young children giggled and young adults called out to one another, some with excitement in their voices, some with urgency.

The deep aromas of espresso from the hotel terrace behind Tammy were strong enough to reach her nose, as was the fragrance of the vases filled with lilacs and orchids being sold by the street vendor nearby. The aromas were just as seductive as the lilting vocal sounds of the Italian soprano in the window three stories above.

This was the vacation of a lifetime, and she was happy that it was only half over. Tammy had wandered the crazy maze of streets in Venice and slurped the incredibly fresh flavors of gelato in Florence. She had gazed out at the green rolling hills of Tuscany that swept by the train window as she traveled from town to town, and she had lingered over long, leisurely evenings on stone balconies perched on the cliffsides of the Amalfi Coast, captive to the scent of bougainvillea and vine-ripe grapes that hung from the balustrade.

Italy was dreamy, and she had no trouble concluding – as had millions of tourists before her – that the country was the most romantic place to be.

Well, at least for most people.

Tammy couldn't dismiss the reality that of all the things she had seen and done while rambling across the regions of Italy – that in this land known for romance and love – she was still alone, and had not even sampled a single romantic moment except for those in her imagination.

The night before, she had sat at a table in the Piazza Navona, a perfect sunset place to be and a favorite spot for visitors and Romans alike while in the city. Despite its local fame, most Americans seem not to find it, but Italian lovers huddled together to share whispered promises in the shadow of Bernini's fountain, and this drew Tammy to the cobbled streets of this particular piazza.

She sat for three hours in a café, watched the twilight slip away and yield to twinkling stars above. She sipped a cold Negroni – a cocktail of Campari, gin, and vermouth that would normally have been too strong for her. She nibbled at the bowl of olives and marinated carrot spears, and inhaled the fragrance of garlic and fennel that coated the little orbs. And she listened to the mandolin music that carried faintly from the dining room behind her.

Alone.

Tammy hadn't come to Italy to find romance but she would have been open to the idea. She was not particularly needy, but the wine, the food, the music in this country – not to mention the brilliant palette of extraordinary scenery that ranged from Medieval castles to verdant hills to post-modern architecture – could put a buzz in anyone with starry-eyed thoughts.

So, after a wonderful but platonic vacation in Italy, she planned to take home many memories of the non-romantic type. That is, until this one moment when it all seemed to change.

Her mind was drawn back to the present and back at the Piazza della Repubblica. With her eyes closed and face tilted toward the warming effect of the sun, she was enjoying a trance-like state when a voice brought her out of it.

"It's warm, no?"

Tammy opened her eyes and turned toward the man's voice. With the sun above casting narrow shadows about, his face was sunlit and easy to see. He had a warm, kind smile, and Tammy smiled back. His blue-hazel eyes were bright, and his dark curly hair cascaded down his forehead. The deep brown beard and mustache were cropped close to his face, and his luxuriously tanned skin crinkled when he smiled at her.

"Um, yes," she replied with a pause. Not a facile response, so, she gave it another try.

"I've been enjoying the warmth of the afternoon." Then, after a momentary pause, "And the scenery here at the fountain makes it a complete experience."

"*Sì*," he said. "It is the Fountain of the Naiads, *la Fontana delle Naiadi*. Did you know that?"

She shook her head.

"Naiads were Greek nymphs," he said, then laughed. "Yes, well, I laugh because they are of Greek creation, but still, here, they are Roman."

"Why nymphs?" Tammy asked. For Americans, the word had pleasurable connotations.

"They are little goddesses," he replied, using his hands to suggest something diminutive. "Here, the naiads look after our fountain, to protect the water and the people who depend upon it."

Okay, so pleasure wasn't their first duty.

"I'm Tammy," she said, extending her hand. He took it and held it warmly for a moment longer than was necessary. But it felt too good for her to pull away from.

"I don't know the name 'Tammy.' But it is American, no?"

"My name is actually Tamara, but everyone calls me Tammy."

He shrugged a little shrug. "But I like the sound of Tamara," he responded. "You should tell this 'everyone' that your name is too beautiful to shorten."

She felt a tingle zing down her back.

"I am Giorgio."

Dinner with Julie

March 2017

"Giorgio? Mom, really?"

Julie was never good as disguising her thoughts through careful modulation of her voice. She came across as both surprised and disappointed, maybe even a bit indelicate in her willingness to doubt me.

"I wasn't a young girl, Julie." Somehow, I felt like I had to defend myself and my time with Giorgio. Julie sat back against the chair and tapped her fork on the plate; she seemed ready to offer some 'grown up' advice to her mother.

"Mom, was that his real name?"

Okay, so that *really* set me off. I had many fond memories of my relationship with Giorgio and how it had matured and developed, but Julie – with no knowledge yet – acted like I needed a lecture about avoiding swarthy Italians approaching me on a street in Rome.

Hmmm. When I thought about it in those terms, I had to laugh a bit myself.

"Yes, Julie, that was his real name. But there's so much more. Can I tell you about him?"

She paused her fork-tapping and focused on me as I proceeded to tell the story of how I met Giorgio so many years ago and how we fell in love.

Piazza della Repubblica, Rome

March 1985

Tamara shook Giorgio's hand and looked into his eyes. The bright color of his iris was amplified by the white surrounding them, which made his eyes seem even more alive set against the bronze glow of his skin.

They talked for some time about their lives – they were both thirty-two years old, both college educated – who they were and what they did for a living.

"I'm an architect," Giorgio revealed in an offhand, unimposing way.

"I'm a CPA," she replied. "That's certified public accountant," she responded.

He laughed that gentle, smiling laugh of his.

"*Sì, sì.* I know what a CPA is. I have one – no, two! – for my company. So," he paused, "you are good with numbers?"

Tamara shrugged her shoulders in an easy reply to the question, and added, "But so are you. You're an architect. I'm sure you're good with numbers, too."

"Yes, well, not like you are. If an architect doesn't like the way the numbers add up, he just erases the line and moves it somewhere else."

His voice was strong but not loud, and he expressed himself with twinkling eyes, hand gestures, and a wink now and then when he was making fun of something, especially himself. There was something so casual and easy-going about Giorgio; and Tamara wondered for a moment why he stopped to speak to a stranger at the fountain. But then she realized that his relaxed demeanor was a simple presentation for a confident, poised man – a public self that held his self-assurance in check while engaging with people.

One of the things they didn't talk about was their families, at least not at first. Tamara could feel a certain reserve in Giorgio – or was she projecting her own on him – as if they wanted to remain just two people sitting at a fountain in Rome for a while longer. As if mention of parents, siblings – spouses? – might ruin the moment. She wasn't married back then and she sneaked a look at Giorgio's ring finger. No jewelry there, and no sign of a tan line.

He didn't ask how long she would be staying in Rome. She waited for the question; it seemed like a natural segue in their discussion, natural for an American tourist to be asked. Their conversation kept her mind too busy to focus on that, but she recalled thinking back later and wondering why Giorgio wasn't interested in that point about her vacation. Maybe he thought it was trite, as in a gigolo asking a single American woman traveling alone, "so, how long will you be in town?" Maybe he didn't want to know because they were really just having a little talk by a fountain in Rome on a sunny afternoon. Nothing serious.

After a while, Giorgio looked down at the street, then surveyed the cars sweeping by. It seemed like he was bringing the conversation to an end, and wondering how to get up and move on. Then he stood and, slapping his hands on his thighs, said he would have to go. But he didn't move.

"I am very glad to meet you, Tamara." He paused, looking for the next thing to say.

"Yes, me too," she said. Tamara was also at a loss for words.

Giorgio turned slightly toward the traffic and smiled back at her.

"I hope you enjoy this lovely city."

"There's no question that I will. And I have."

He turned full on to the street and took a few steps away, then stopped. He turned back to her with a wan smile. Waving once more, he turned back away and took another few steps before stopping again.

"Tamara," he called out, but then he ran out of words. After a few seconds, he came back to her, sat down on the fountain wall again and peered into her eyes.

"Tamara, would you be interested in joining me for a glass of wine?"

Dinner with Julie

March 2017

Julie's gaze had softened a bit as I told her the story. My memory of Giorgio, and maybe my telling of how I met him, seemed less threatening than she first assumed. I think I even saw a glint of romance in my daughter's eyes as she concentrated on my account.

"Giorgio was a perfect gentleman." I felt obliged to reassure Julie at the first. "Despite his obvious self-assurance, he was not forward. He was gentle and thoughtful throughout."

"Was he as nice as dad?" Julie asked. I always knew that if I told her about Giorgio her first question would be to compare him to her own father. The slight hesitation in her voice brought this dilemma home.

"Both of them are wonderful. But they don't have to be the same." I had no qualms about defending my dear husband, Ted. He was a wonderful husband and father and, more importantly, my best friend. I wouldn't trade him for the world. And I still ached for losing him.

But, then again, there's Giorgio. And I was having trouble explaining to Julie how I felt about him.

"He had such an easy smile, and he listened to me when I talked," I began. Giorgio's physical features were etched into my memory, but I didn't think describing his physique or handsome face would make this any easier for Julie.

"I was a young woman," I reminded her, "but still a woman." Why I felt the need to point out my femininity – or was it my sexuality? – to my daughter didn't occur to me at that moment. Whenever I was with Giorgio, I was at ease and my words flowed without having to measure them, and it seemed that the same affect held power over me even when I was only talking about him.

"I suppose you went with Giorgio for that glass of wine," Julie asked, eyes cast down and one finger tracing circles on the tabletop.

Ristorante Farini, Rome

March 1985

Giorgio walked with Tamara to the other side of the piazza, stepping quickly between swerving taxicabs, and pointed out a little trattoria snuggled into the corner. They squeezed between the waist-high, arched metal bars that kept the cars from careening over the curb and wiping out the sidewalk crowd of thirsty customers.

A young waiter perched on the doorstep of the establishment called out to Giorgio and pointed to a small table for two on the edge of the café, and they slipped into the chairs.

"So, you're a regular here?" she teased.

Giorgio shrugged his shoulders and smiled.

"Italians like wine, and we especially like to enjoy it in the shade of a sidewalk café. And, yes" – did she detect a slight blush on his cheekbones? – "I come back to Ristorante Farini often."

"My office is just over there," he said with a wave of the hand. The gesture didn't indicate a particular building but sufficed to convey that he worked in the neighborhood.

Tamara ordered an Arneis from the Ceretto winery, he a Castello Volpaia Chianti Classico. The waiter who had hailed Giorgio reappeared quickly with both glasses, a shallow bowl of marinated olives both black and green and oiled with an oregano-scented oil, and a tall thick-walled tumbler filled with twisted breadsticks redolent of sesame and rosemary.

They sipped their wine and munched on the savory snacks while exploring more facts about their lives and plans. Giorgio had attended the *Università di*

Firenze but was hired by a firm in Rome. He regretted leaving his beloved Florence – "the art, the architecture, and the gardens!" He said he missed all that.

"And the pretty ladies?" Tamara couldn't pass up the chance to tease him. His manner made it easy to assume a familiar way with him.

Another slight shrug and a smile. Giorgio looked down at the table, then back up into her eyes, and replied.

"*Sì*, but the ladies in Roma are also quite wonderful."

She pondered his choice of "wonderful" over "beautiful." It seemed to her that Giorgio was a man who would judge a woman on more than her skin, legs, and hair.

As the late afternoon wore on and night began to fall, they moved on to other wines. Giorgio was shocked that Tamara had never had Prosecco, a pleasant yet uncomplicated sparkling wine from northern Italy.

"I've tasted Asti Spumante," she mentioned, "but that's too sweet."

"No, no, no," he said with a wagging finger. "Prosecco." Then he turned to the waiter and repeated the word to him, adding "*una bottiglia*" – a bottle – of LaMarca.

Food followed the Prosecco, first *crostini alla napolitana*, a dish very much like *bruschetta*, but the bread slices are buttered first, then topped with mozzarella, diced tomatoes, anchovies and oregano before broiling. With their taste buds properly awakened, Giorgio ordered *necci*, a type of flatbread made from chestnut flour, topped with ricotta and chopped basil leaves.

The Prosecco died a happy death with those two courses, but Giorgio was not finished yet. Signaling the waiter with an upraised hand, he ordered a bottle of Vietti Barbera, telling Tamara that it was a luscious wine but not as dry or as robust – with that word, he acted out a weightlifter's pose – as the typical Italian red wines.

"For those who like white wine," he said, "Barbera is easier to take."

"I'm not a wimp," she protested, and he laughed. "I mean, I drink red wine," Tamara explained, "I just felt like a white wine first." Then she was the one to laugh, a tiny bit embarrassed that she had resorted to self-defense. Or maybe she was a tiny bit high on wine. Or something.

Before the Barbera arrived, he ordered a bowl of *giuget* for each of them.

"They're little squares of dough, but not stuffed like *ravioli*," he said, using his thumbs and index fingers to approximate the size. "Here, they toss them with oil, melted butter, herbs, and pancetta, sometimes sausage. You'll like it."

Her head was swimming, either from wine, food, or these glorious descriptions of the dinner they were sharing.

That's when it hit her: She was having dinner with Giorgio; it wasn't just a glass of wine. They were so comfortable together that neither considered ending the event, so one glass led to another, and one plate of food led to another.

Before Tamara could protest – like there was any chance she would – the bottle of Barbera arrived and the *giuget* was served.

Dinner with Julie

March 2017

"Sounds like a long meal," Julie said in a near whisper. There was a bit of worry in her voice, a reluctance to ask when that meal actually ended, but there was also a note of envy.

"It was an easy conversation. We had lots to talk about," I added, although even then, on that wonderful evening, I couldn't say what we actually talked about. We just talked.

Julie stood up and collected our salad plates and disappeared into the kitchen for a minute. When she returned to the table, she was carrying our dinner, broiled chicken breasts, some small grilled halves of potatoes, and a side of broccoli tossed with sautéed diced onions. As we resumed eating, my mind went back to that night in 1985.

Telling this story to Julie brought warm memories back and the words came so simply to me. But I paused when it dawned on me that my pleasure in telling might not match my daughter's trepidation in hearing stories about another man not her father.

"Remember," I said abruptly, this was all before I met your father."

"Did you see Giorgio again?"

"You mean after that dinner? Of course," then my cheeks turned red when I considered how that must have sounded.

"On that trip to Rome," Julie filled in for me, drawing out her words for emphasis.

"Yes." A moment passed, and I added, "and again later, twice. On other trips to Rome."

Julie melted a bit at that, as she realized that this thing between me and Giorgio had some depth and duration. She set her fork down, crossed her arms on the table, and focused on me with a look of love that convinced me that she was now on my side.

I gulped first before continuing.

"And again. Six months ago."

Her gasp was all-too audible.

Basilica di San Pietro in Vincoli, Rome

1985

Giorgio walked Tamara back to her hotel that evening, not far from the little restaurant where they spent so many hours. She was feeling the effects of the wine, but still in control of her faculties. She wasn't going to allow herself to fall victim to the riskier urges of this budding romance.

But then, she had nothing to fear from Giorgio.

He walked her into the lobby of the hotel and, before turning to go, asked if he might see her again the next day. He still hadn't asked how long Tamara would be in Rome but, at that moment, she would have cancelled her flight if it was scheduled for the next morning.

"*Sì*," she responded. Something possessed her to use the Italian word to accede to his request.

Tamara woke up early and showered, then dressed and went to the lobby on the first floor for breakfast. She piled several slices of cheese and prosciutto on her plate, added two fresh-baked rolls still warm from the oven and a dollop of *crème fraiche* and capers. Staring at her plate, she marveled at how her hunger had returned so soon after that repast the night before.

Returning to her room, Tamara gave a little more thought to how to dress for the day. Giorgio said he wanted to show her a special basilica often overlooked by tourists, so she would need to have on something modest. But she assumed they would find other entertainments during the day and the forecast for warm temperatures suggested that she prepare for that also.

About ten o'clock, Tamara went down to the lobby where Giorgio was already waiting for her. His version of casual clothes – like most Italians – was more stylish than Americans' version, but still he looked comfortable. She giggled when she saw that, below his neatly pressed slacks, he wore sporty sneakers with blue sides, white rubber soles, and yellow ribbing on the sides.

"Okay," he said, holding up one hand palm out. "They're comfortable, right? Don't you Americans wear these shoes?"

"Yes, we do," Tamara said through the fingers covering her mouth. "But I didn't think you did."

Giorgio's lips pursed tightly, but not in anger. Then they opened in a broad smile and he held out his arm for her to take. Looping her hand through his crooked elbow seemed so European that it made Tamara forget his Nikes.

They walked and walked. Giorgio pointed out sights that she knew of and had read about, and other things she had never seen. He may have been from Florence, but he seemed extraordinarily proud of the Eternal City and adopted the life and culture of Rome as if it were his birthplace.

An easy hour passed that way and Tamara could tell that they weren't walking in a direct line to anywhere. Giorgio was circumnavigating the sites in this section of Rome as if he didn't have any particular place to go, as if he would rather show off the beauty and style of the city and as if they had all the time in the world to do so.

"I'm sorry," he said suddenly, stopping in the middle of a block of ancient buildings. "I'm boring you, aren't I?"

"No, no, you're not. I'm very interested." And, actually, she was. His narrative on the history of Rome mingled with the biographies of the great artists and statesmen of the city, and these blended right in with his architect's description of the buildings. His sonorous voice and the evident excitement in his telling were captivating.

"But you're not saying anything," he protested. "I'm not letting you talk."

Tamara put her hand gently on his arm. "Giorgio, how can I talk about this city any better than you can? I am truly enjoying myself. Please," she added, "let's go on."

So, they did. Although, now, Giorgio would more often pause in his running account and ask her what she thought of something.

They finally arrived at the little church he had told her about – the *Basilica di San Pietro in Vincoli.* Not "little" exactly, but out of the way and, just as Giorgio had said, not frequented by many tourists. There was a little piazza in front and the church itself had mostly non-descript doors, but once inside it took on the true grandeur of an Italian basilica.

She knew from her own reading that Italians are most interested in the décor and beauty on the insides of their buildings. This was obvious in their own homes, which could have simple flat stone façades but interiors adorned with lace curtains, cut crystal vases, and carved tables and hutches inlaid with multiple grains of wood. The outside-inside dichotomy was a bit less traditional when it came to grand churches like St. Peter's Basilica in Rome, but Tamara wasn't surprised when she saw that the simple exterior of this "little church" hid some exquisite decorations inside.

Directly ahead she saw the ornate altar and a large reliquary slightly below floor level. But to the right of the altar was a sculpture that, when she laid eyes on it, left her speechless. She had seen photographs of Michelangelo's *Moses* before, the incredibly lifelike marble carving about which even its creator had uttered "why don't you speak" when he gazed upon it. And she knew it was attached to the tomb of Pope Julius II, an astonishingly historic artistic flourish for this little church. But Tamara had never been this close to it, and she had no idea that Giorgio would steer her there.

"*Magnifico*," was his single word to describe the towering sculpture, and Tamara could only nod her head in agreement. They stood before it for several minutes, mentally untangling the curves and edges of marble that Michelangelo had deftly carved. While she tried to take in the wonder of it all, Giorgio tapped her on the arm.

"There is something else here, but maybe not as wonderful as the *Moses*." He pointed with his left hand at the reliquary in front of the altar.

Italians are fond of their relics, more so than most other Catholics who count on bits of bone, hair, and dried droplets of blood from saints to bestow blessings upon them in times of need. The reliquaries in Italy contain many body parts, from mummified heads and hands to questionable claims of wood splinters from the "real" cross. A tour company could offer a relic tour of the country – even just Rome itself – and would be able to remain in business for decades.

They turned toward the reliquary that Giorgio pointed to and Tamara saw a loose chain of metal links draped over hooks in the ceiling of the glass box.

"*San Pietro*, right?" Giorgio offered. St. Peter, yes, she nodded, acknowledging the name of the church.

"*In vincoli*," he said, pointing to the chain in the reliquary.

Her Italian was modest and that word made no sense to her, but he was pointing to the chain.

"It is said that these were the chains used to hold St. Peter when he was taken by the Romans after Jesus was arrested."

Tamara's eyes went wide when she considered the possibility. If the story was true, these were about as momentous as any relic could get. But it could not be, she thought. It couldn't; could it?

Giorgio shrugged his shoulders as if he had heard her unasked question.

She stood there for a long time, studying the display. Tamara had been raised Catholic and believed most of the stories told about by the ancients, until doubts crept in later in her life. She had not abandoned the faith, and wondered at times if she would ever return to it – and under what circumstances – but she couldn't dismiss the historic significance of this chain, if the story supporting it was true.

They walked past the reliquary, then turned left to pass the pews and exit the church through the towering doors where they had entered. The bright sunshine outside brought Tamara back to the present, but she was still entranced with the *Moses* who sat majestically at the edge of the pope's tomb.

Enoteca Buccone, Rome

March 1985

Giorgio donned sunglasses and Tamara shielded her eyes from the glare with one hand and searched her bag for sunglasses with the other. He looked left, then right, as if he was trying to decide what to explore next, then looked at his wristwatch.

"Ah, so, of course," he said softly, almost to himself. He held his arm out for Tamara to take, and they turned right toward the street at the bottom of the steps that lead down from the basilica.

"I know a perfect little place for... what do you say in America? Lunch?"

She nodded, knowing that he had a good command of English but he enjoyed playing with her.

"Here it is called *pranzo*, *sì*?" she countered.

Giorgio's eyes brightened and his smile spread.

"*Sì*, yes, of course!" His voice carried a note of pleasure that Tamara had at least some Italian words at her disposal. He seemed especially pleased that the words she knew had to do with food.

They covered only a few blocks when he pointed toward a door sunken into the front of a stone building, a darkened door that, once they were inside, led to a long, narrow room. There were softly illuminated chandeliers dotting the ribbon of ceiling above and tables arranged along the two sides of the room, leaving just enough space between them to allow a single-file of customers or waiters. Snug enough that when a customer going in met a waiter coming out of the kitchen, they both had to step between crowded tables to let the other pass.

The elaborately papered walls rose at least fifteen feet to ancient stone arches that crisscrossed the ceiling, bearing a chandelier at each of its crosses. There were no windows in the room since it was sandwiched between two other buildings crowding this street, but the dim light of incandescent bulbs created a cozy atmosphere, an oasis from the sunny outside.

Tables bore white cloths set with only vaguely polished utensils. It wasn't that they were burnished or unkempt, but the knives, forks, and teaspoons looked like their surroundings – like they had been there for centuries.

Giorgio and Tamara were directed to a table midway down the room, next to a couple on one side and a mother, father, and two children on the other. The first set of neighbors talked quietly among themselves; the second table sported more boisterous sounds rung in with the incessant spoon-tapping of the pre-school age boy.

"Valerio's is more traditionally Roman, not like Farini, where the owner likes to present food from around the country. Here, in Valerio's, the food is Roman."

"As in Lazio, the region, or Rome, the city?" she asked.

"Oh, no," Giorgio responded, wagging his finger for emphasis. "Roman. All through this part of Italy, meat and *verdure*...um, how do you say...um..." he used his hands to indicate something but it was too obscure for Tamara to make out.

"As, like, *zucchini, tomate, asparagi...*"

"You mean vegetables," she ventured.

"*Sì*, yes, vegetables, *verdure*. So, those from Lazio use many ingredients, and have many ways to eat them. But in Rome, a meal is not considered complete without having meat. And pasta!"

He added that last thing with gusto, and Tamara was sure that Giorgio was at the start of another feast.

They scanned the menu written entirely in Italian. She could figure out most of it and when she stumbled on a word or phrase, Giorgio would look over her menu, put his finger on the item, and explain what she was looking at. *Garum* sounded interesting until she discovered that it was a sauce made of fish guts.

"They don't actually make that kind of *garum* anymore," he told her, conspicuously worried about ruining her appetite with talk of this ancient concoction.

"That's from the old days," he continued. "In Valerio's, they use the meat of the white fish and combine it with bright green olive oil, herbs and a little salt. It's very good," he added, to cast her doubts away.

Giorgio ordered *fave con pecorino*, fava beans that had been drizzled with olive oil then served with chips of pecorino cheese and bits of salami. Tamara settled for *misticanze* once she recognized that it was a tossed green salad reminiscent of home. But the salads she ate back in America didn't have diced fennel, balsamic vinegar, toasted halves of hazelnuts, and bits of smoked mozzarella in them.

"Good, yes?" Giorgio asked after a few bites. He was always properly polite, but he ate his food with only barely controlled gusto.

Of course, there was wine. Instead of ordering by the glass, Giorgio suggested a bottle. A bottle! In the middle of the day. All she could think was "oh, my!"

A Bongiovanni Dolcetto was brought to the table. Glasses were already there – what Roman eats without wine? – and the waiter swung into action. Pulling a corkscrew from his pocket, he extracted the blade and quickly severed the head of the capsule on the bottletop, exposing the cork but leaving the shroud of the decorated capsule around the throat of the bottle. In one motion, he reversed the tool and spun the sharpened worm into the soft cork. Without setting the bottle down but resting the butt of it on his hip, he jerked on the corkscrew and the wine suddenly emitted a soft "pop" as if it was introducing itself to the table.

A short taste was poured for Giorgio's approval, then the wine was poured into their glasses. Tamara held hers up and Giorgio tipped his toward her, clinking the polished rims together, smiling back and nodding his head. She let the wine glide across her tongue and down her throat and – as easily as that – Tamara decided that she could definitely live life as an Italian.

"Do you know why it is the custom to tap glasses together?" he asked.

"Because the ancients thought that wine contained evil spirits," she said with confidence. "They tip and clink their glasses to cast off the demons."

Giorgio set his glass down on the table, leaned back, and gave her his proudest smile.

"You are a very smart American."

"Don't underestimate us," she warned him with a grin.

His eyebrows raised in a show of respect, and that smile reappeared.

Giorgio ordered *curiole*, an egg pasta shaped like *tagliatelle*, with asparagus tips and parmesan sprinkled over it. Tamara decided to pass on the first course, protesting that she was too-soon approaching her limit. But she did pour another glass of the Dolcetto.

For the next course, he requested *guanciale,* cured pork jowl that was more aromatic and beautiful than she anticipated. Tamara took a slightly more conservative approach, choosing a version of comfort food: *abbacchio alla cacciatora,* a casserole dish that included lamb, garlic, rosemary, and white wine, brought to life with a dash of red pepper flakes.

They passed the afternoon over that table and Tamara never thought to look at the time. They continued their running conversation about all things large and small. They talked society and its rules, art and architecture, and Italians' *la dolce vita.*

"You know, life isn't all sweet for us," Giorgio commented, referring to famous phrase about "the sweet life."

Appraising the display of food and wine they consumed for lunch, Tamara flashed a doubting smile.

"Oh, yes, that's what we would prefer – the sweet life – but we have to work just like you do in the States. But for us, one thing is different," he said with an upraised finger pointed to the ceiling. "Not *la dolce vita,* but *la dolce far niente* – The 'sweetness of having nothing to do.' "

He put down his fork, took a sip of wine, and leaned back in his chair as if declaring a small but significant victory.

"Americans strive to succeed, some say they live to work," he said.

Tamara shook her head in disagreement.

"No, that's an exaggeration," she countered.

"Oh, sure," he continued, not deterred. "You will protest and say that's not true. You will say that you 'work to live.' Americans have memorized that phrase. And they try to rest and to enjoy life. But for Italians – *la dolce far niente* – it's a part of every day. Our long, lingering meals, that glass of wine on the balcony at sunset, the *passeggiata* each evening when we gather with friends and family to walk and talk around the city's streets and *piazze.* We don't have to insist on those interludes in life. They're always there. They *are* life for us."

Giorgio said all this without a tone of reprimand, and certainly not like he was trying to prove something to her. But it was clear that he wanted to explain how the Italian style of living was more humane, and more human. Tamara resorted to the American way of agreeing.

She raised her glass and said, "I'll drink to that."

Enoteca Buccone, Rome

March 1985

When they finally emerged from Valerio's, it was late afternoon and time to walk off the giant meal they had consumed. Giorgio took the reins again and guided Tamara down wide streets and narrow alleys, pointing out the architectural designs and carved shrines that were etched into the corners of the buildings.

He even pointed out the best galleries where tourists were known to shop for copies of the Italian masterpiece paintings. And a tiny shop with a brightly lit window where gleaming gems and gold necklaces were on display.

"The streets in my home of Firenze are, of course, the best place to buy gold, but..." he shrugged and paused for a beat, "this one's not too bad either."

With no warning, Giorgio turned right and stepped through the door into a wine shop, the Enoteca Buccone, leaving Tamara briefly befuddled on the sidewalk. She recovered quickly and went inside in search of Giorgio, whom she found among the tall stacks of wine bottles. Enoteca Buccone is famous throughout Italy for its expansive collection of wine, and it didn't surprise Tamara that Giorgio knew it, or that he knew the owner personally.

Francesco Buccone could be mistaken for one of the clerks in his shop, minding the ladder that reached the upper racks as casually as he swept up the floor when bits of bread or *grissini* fell there. But his knowledge of the wine was superior to anyone who worked in his shop or, perhaps, anywhere in the city.

"*Buon giorno*," Giorgio said clasping Francesco's hand. "This is Tamara," he said stepping to the side and introducing her.

"*Buon giorno. Mi piacere*," their host said. "My pleasure."

Giorgio also knew the catalog of wines in the store, and didn't wait to be directed by Francesco.

"The Brunello di Montalcino is my favorite wine," he said, pulling a bottle of Poggio Antico from its cradle on the shelf.

"You mean your favorite Italian wine, right?" Tamara asked.

"What?" he said with a feigned smile. "Other people make wine too? That's marvelous! I should try some one day."

Francesco took in this banter with a grin, knowing well Giorgio's loyalty to all things Italian.

Under Francesco's careful eye, Giorgio and Tamara drew samples of more wines standing on the counter next to the iPad-like cash register.

"*Che cos'è?*" Giorgio asked, pointing to the brightly lit screen. "What is this?"

Francesco offered only an impish grin, but admitted that he had to convert from the ancient brass cash register to this new device. "*È piu facile,*" he said – "It's easier."

"*Beh,*" was Giorgio's little retort, carrying a slightly dismissive tone.

They spent nearly an hour tasting wines before Giorgio selected a handful of bottles to buy. Tamara wondered if these wines would appear at their next repast – he hadn't asked but she was already anticipating another glorious meal with Giorgio.

Out on the street, with Tamara still wondering where these wines would end up, Giorgio said softly, "It's not polite to taste a man's wines then not buy anything. Your hotel has a rooftop terrace, no?"

Tamara nodded yes, although her skin glowed warm with the next thought.

"So, here," he said, handing the bag to her. We are too far from my home," Giorgio continued, using that same vague wave of the hand without indicating where, in fact, he did live.

"You can keep these in your hotel and, perhaps, you will invite me to sit on the terrace this evening and enjoy this wine by starlight."

Tamara still hadn't said anything about the length of her stay in Rome, but Giorgio's offer seemed to be a subtle invitation to stay.

"Yes, that would be wonderful" she said, taking the bag with her hand as Giorgio hailed a taxi.

Dinner with Julie

March 2017

"Mom," Julie interrupted my story. "I don't think of you as drinking wine. I mean, I know you do, but Dad and you didn't have much of it around."

"Yes, well, but you know I liked it," I replied. We just didn't have it at the same frequency as the Italians do."

"Like Giorgio," Julie added.

I had to smile at her. My daughter wavered between protecting me and wondering aloud at what she didn't know about her mother. What she was finding out on this particular evening.

I hadn't eaten much of the chicken on my plate, absorbed as I was with the story. So, I turned to the food for a few moments while my mind wandered back to Giorgio, then to my husband.

Ted and I had been married for twenty-six years, until he succumbed to cancer two years ago. Twenty-four of those years were shared with our only child, Julie, and we were a constant threesome. It was a perfect life, and I never wanted for anything. And I never thought about Giorgio.

At least not until Ted passed. I guess I spent moments of loneliness, and when that happens people begin to reach back into the past. I didn't think of Giorgio as my replacement for Ted; that wouldn't have worked and I never would have given up my husband. But my time with Giorgio those many years ago seemed so different, so apart from my real life. And I wondered why he didn't show up that day years ago; why, after seeing each other for so long, he just disappeared.

After several visits to Rome and long, serious talks about our future, Giorgio was suddenly out of my life, and I was alone again, sitting at the edge of the Fountain of the Naiads.

Until six months ago.

I didn't know how to explain all this to Julie without her wondering whether I preferred this mysterious man in Rome to her father. I only barely thought I understood it myself.

Colosseum, Rome

March 1985

"It's the perfect way to see Roma," Giorgio said.

He had guided Tamara to the upper tier of the Colosseum just as the sun started its descent toward the horizon. The massive hulk of buildings on the Palatine Hill were darkened by the sun that was setting behind them, while the light played through the ruined arches of the Forum and cast a reddish-reflection off the buildings to the east of their perch.

"At different times," Giorgio explained to Tamara, "the officials in Rome have allowed tourists to come here in the evenings, and at other times, no!" he ended with emphasis on the final word. He explained that access to the Colosseum was always considered a treasured moment when visiting Rome, but the government believed the two-thousand-year old theatre should be spared frequent traffic.

Giorgio said he liked to watch the sunset from there, a time when he was able to think about life in the Eternal City, in Italy itself – and to consider his own existence.

"But, tonight," he said with glee, pointing his right index finger in the air, "it is only March and the sun sets too early."

Tamara couldn't keep up with this thinking, but laughed at his enthusiasm. Crinkling her eyebrows and displaying a look of confusion, she called for a more thorough explanation from him.

"The sun sets so early in March, and our *cena* – dinner – would not have been enjoyed yet, so we won't be ending our evening in this glorious amphitheatre. After we are done here, we shall eat!"

The prospect of another meal could always produce an enthusiastic response from Giorgio, and this evening was no different.

"Where would you like to eat?" he asked Tamara, who could only raise her eyebrows and give a little shrug, signaling both an openness to suggestion and total absence of any particular recommendation.

"You choose," she said, knowing full well that Giorgio had a greater command of the venues than she did.

"*D'accordo*," he said – "agreed" – and he swung into action. Taking Tamara by the hand, he guided her back down the steps to the lowest level, turning only once to bid "*arrivederci*" to the sun, and out onto the Piazza del Colosseo at street level.

Tamara still enjoyed Giorgio's rapid-paced conversation but was now familiar enough with him that she didn't let him dominate their talk. Arm in arm they walked up the Via dei Fori Imperiale to Via Cavour, where Giorgio quickly chose a restaurant at the corner, called Mario's, shaking hands with a head waiter who was obviously already an acquaintance.

Tamara and Giorgio were taken to a table in the back of the restaurant, one that offered a royal view of the dining room. The table sat on a shallow platform that put them about eight inches above the floor level, and Tamara felt like they were appointed the "don" of the evening with their oversight of the clientele clustered at tables around them.

When the last rays of the setting sun disappeared from the single stained-glass window at the front of the restaurant, the lights in the hall were also dimmed slightly, so Tamara could see that despite their lofty perch, they enjoyed a special privacy in that corner of the room.

The head waiter arrived with a bottle of sparkling water and another bottle of red wine, each clutched between two fingers of his left hand. With little ceremony, he plunked the water bottle down, unscrewed the cap, and filled two tumblers full on the table. Then, with a bit more poise and expertise, he showcased the wine.

Tamara didn't remember seeing Giorgio order anything yet, and she wondered whether this was just the same wine he had every time he dined at Mario's, or whether the waiter was taking charge of the meal for them.

The waiter turned the bottle around for them to see, and Tamara read Barbaresco in big letters. Looking again, she saw above it Produttori del Barbaresco. She was familiar with this type of wine, but had only tasted it once or twice. And she had never had the wine from Produttori del Barbaresco, but the waiter seemed proud of being able to offer it. He extracted the tiny blade from the edge of the corkscrew and quickly severed the capsule from the bottle, then spun the screw into the cork. With a quick tug, the cork popped out and the waiter proceeded to pour half-glasses for each of them. This time, there was no sample offered for her or Giorgio and Tamara was coming to the conclusion that this type of service was what the Italians refer to as *stile familiare*, which sometimes meant "homemade" but was also used to refer to home style, or family-style service when used in restaurants.

Giorgio and Tamara took thirsty sips of the wine – far more exquisite than anything she expected for family-style service – and savored its texture and aromas before returning to their conversation.

"Why did you pick Rome?" Giorgio asked suddenly, a bit out of context.

Tamara considered the question for a moment, took another sip of wine, and then put her glass down gently. She folded her arms on the edge of the table and began.

"I had come here first while in high school," she said.

"With your parents?"

"No, as a student. We were on a student exchange trip. There were ten of us, Americans, who came to live with the families of the ten Italian youths who went to live with our families in the United States.

"Then I came again on a short vacation with friends, during college."

"I guess that means you liked it?" Giorgio queried.

"Yes, of course. I also returned once more, after college, with some more friends. Now, it's your turn. Why did you choose Rome?" She knew Giorgio had accepted a job there, but was there anything else?

"After I graduated from university," he said, "I had the chance to extend my study, in New York and in Paris."

"Sounds like an envious choice," she interjected.

"*Sì, ma no*," he added, peering into his wine glass as he swirled its contents. "I have cousins in New York and I knew I could live with them, but my work requires that I stay here, in Italy."

Tamara wasn't sure why his work as an architect would require him to remain in Italy, but she didn't pry.

"And Paris?"

"Yes, of course, it's beautiful." Giorgio paused a long moment, a hint that there was something else at work.

"Did she love you?" Tamara ventured, startling even herself at the *non sequitur.*

Giorgio didn't look up from the red liquid in his glass, but let out a gentle laugh, more like a huff.

"*Sì*," but when he looked up at Tamara, his eyes glowed as if she were the center of his story, and her nerves tingled again.

No menus arrived at the table and yet the food began to show up.

First, there was a platter of bread, marinated vegetables, and the ubiquitous and multi-hued olives. There was *crostini alla ponticiana,* little slices of bread that had been slathered with butter and then fried, then covered with thinly sliced prosciutto and sautéed mushrooms. This was served alongside *filone,* long crusty loaves of bread. There was *carciofi ripieni* – stuffed artichokes – and *cazzimperio* – an assortment of raw vegetables served alongside a squat bowl of bright green olive oil, with a sprinkling of rock salt and freshly ground black pepper.

After working through that platter, the waiter came to inspect the contents of the wine bottle. Holding it up to the dim light of the bulb above the table, he clicked his tongue and shook his head, indicating disappointment that it was taking these lovers so long to finish the wine. From the side table, he served the soup he had carried over. It was *stracciatella alla romana,* a hot broth riddled with swirls of beaten egg, topped with shavings of parmesan cheese and a sprinkle of nutmeg in the center.

When the waiter stepped back from the table, Giorgio turned the conversation back to Tamara.

"So, now, you have come back to Rome alone? How is that so?"

Tamara paused before answering, not certain in her head about how this had taken place. Yes, she had come before, with fellow students and friends, but this time, at thirty-two and in her particular place in her career, she felt like she needed to travel. Most of her friends were now married and in the early stages of raising kids. She had not taken that path yet, so there were fewer choices of whom to travel with. And she explained that to Giorgio.

But that only explained why she was alone, not why she was in Rome. And Giorgio went back to that.

"But Rome...Italy. What about Paris, Amsterdam, Stockholm, Vienna...why not China?"

"Italy feels good to me. I was drawn back here from my memories, from what I experienced, from what I thought the culture offered me."

"Have you found what you were looking for?"

Tamara didn't know how to answer his question, and wondered whether it was time to venture into the "what are you looking for" arena. And even if it was time, she wasn't sure what to say to Giorgio. But she suspected that her secret was only barely hiding under the surface.

The waiter arrived to rescue her, bearing a platter of *penne all'arrabbiata.* The penne noodle is dressed in a spicy sauce, literally *arrabbiato* – angry – but with a velvety smooth texture and brilliant flavor of spiced tomatoes and diced pancetta. He also delivered another bottle of wine – unasked – and Tamara laughed between bites of the penne.

They completed the two-hour repast with small glasses of Brolio Vin Santo, Tuscany's famous dessert wine made from grapes that are hung to dry and concentrate their juices before crushing and fermentation. After Giorgio paid the bill – Tamara objected, saying she should contribute, but he held up one hand in defense of the suggestion – they stepped out of the restaurant into the cool air of a spring night. Tamara was still dressed in her day clothing which was inadequate for the night, but Giorgio only laughed, apologizing for not having a jacket to give her.

"I would give you the shirt on my back," he teased. She laughed and said, "oh, no, please don't" but couldn't shake the visual of Giorgio without a shirt.

He walked her back to her hotel and, always the gentleman, turned to her at the door and bade her a good night.

"Are you free tomorrow?"

Tamara nodded yes.

"In that case, may I spend some time with you?"

Again, the nod, with a happy smile to accompany it. This time, Giorgio leaned in for a kiss, and Tamara welcomed it.

The Steps of St. Peter's Basilica, Rome

March 1985

Giorgio was sitting on the second step on the promenade outside the Basilica, leaning back on his elbows with his face turned up towards the early morning sun. Tamara was sitting beside him, but paying more attention to the tourists than to the celestial body above.

People were pouring out of buses and as pedestrians across the streets, angling toward the massive doors of the church. The piazza outside is immense and yet, filled with these teeming throngs, it seemed on a human scale. Tamara watched these tourists from every country and race head toward the church, and wondered how many were members of the Catholic Church and how many were merely visitors to this greatest of all attractions in Rome. The Colosseum had witnessed mock battles and human sacrifices to the Roman ego; the Pantheon had served as a spiritual gathering place for pagans, Romans, and early Christians; and the Forum had hosted the glitterati of the ancient city, but these were all monuments to the past. St. Peter's had an enduring and very-present attraction and people came from all over the world to see it.

Except Giorgio.

Tamara looked over at him and he was still there, head tilted back, eyes closed.

"The sun is different here," he said suddenly. Sitting up, he continued, "Well, it's different in Tuscany, too. And in Positano."

Tamara was sure that he could continue rambling like that, naming all the towns and regions of Italy, in his very Giorgio-way, so she stepped in.

"And in New York, and Washington, and Philadelphia."

"*Sì, certo*," he said, his head bobbing in agreement. "But, here, in Italy, it's different."

"Okay, now wait a minute." Tamara decided it was time she defended her country. "The sunshine is wonderful and, yes, it's different here – as it is everywhere – but America is also a wonderful country."

"Yes, it is," Giorgio said, and his words convinced Tamara that he was speaking from direct experience. Knowing that she would ask him about it, Giorgio changed direction. "And I should visit it sometime."

His tone sounded like he was suggesting that he visit her.

He couldn't leave the debate undone, though. Giorgio had to finish their back-and-forth.

"But the sunlight is especially beautiful in my home, in Firenze."

"What makes it so?" Tamara challenged, although she secretly agreed with him.

Giorgio considered the question before answering, then tilted his head back toward the blue heavens above. It seemed like he was about to supply some conclusive evidence, some incontrovertible proof, but he grinned and closed his eyes again.

"I don't know," he admitted, but the smile persisted.

Fori Imperiali, Rome

March 1985

Tamara and Giorgio wandered the streets of Rome and slowly ambled toward the old Roman Forum, the *Fori Imperiali* where the ancient government convened. It had once been an organized cluster of magnificent buildings, towering white columns topped with terracotta roofs, temples to various deities, streets organized to highlight the walk of dignitaries gathering for political debate , and soaring sculptures that capped each building as a testament to the greatness of Rome.

It had been the scene of many historic events, not least of which was the assassination of Julius Caesar in 44 B.C.E. But the Forum, this most Roman of monuments, fell into disrepair with the decline of the Roman Empire, and suffered badly during the Middle Ages. It was sacked by invading armies and ransacked by thieves carting off slabs of marble for other constructions. Fortunately, the modern-day Roman government dedicated considerable resources to restoring and preserving it. Not only was the Forum a spectacular tourist destination, it also represents the glory days of the Roman Republic and the Roman Empire.

Giorgio and Tamara walked down lanes only partially covered with the original stones, past looming columns that once heralded the pre-Christian religions of Rome, and between buildings from whose steps great speeches were delivered. Giorgio pointed to the towering edifice of the Basilica Giulia, the lonely pillars that remained of the Temple of Castor and Pollux, the broad-shouldered Arch of Septimius Severus, and the crumbling steps of Basilica Emilia.

"Right here," Giorgio said, pointing to the ground at their feet. "It was right here that Carlo Fea struck his pick into the ground and began to unearth the ruins of the Roman Forum."

"It was covered over?"

"Well, not by people, but by time. The *Fori Imperiali* had been lost to us until Fea decided to dig down to find it once again."

"Who's he, and when did this happen?"

"About 1803. He was a scientist with a great imagination. His imagination led him to believe that this city..." Giorgio said this with a sweep of his arm, "was still here." And he pointed once again to the ground at their feet.

"1803? Wait," Tamara protested. "How do we know he began that excavation right here?"

"Well, of course, we don't know it was actually right here," Giorgio said with his usual teasing tone, jabbing his right index finger at his feet. "But every story has to have specific details to make it sound real."

Tamara smiled at the typical Giorgio response.

"The work went on for over a hundred years before the buildings could be identified," he continued. "Even now, archeologists continue to scrap away at the dirt and residue and find more ruins below. This area actually includes several centuries of buildings, you understand. The Romans occupied this space for a long time and acknowledged that this Forum was the center of their governmental, religious, and social life. So, buildings were built upon other buildings, government systems changed and were replaced by others, and people came and went.

"Right through here," he added, swinging his arm in a long arc to indicate the broad thoroughfare where they stood, "Right here on the *Via Sacra* was where the conquering Roman armies returned to the city in triumph, and where emperors walked to cheering crowds. And over there," he said, pointing to a low, marble platform beside the Curia, "was where Marc Anthony gave his eulogy to Caesar."

Giorgio's descriptions were so visual that Tamara could imagine the brilliant colors of the city around her: the deep lustrous purple of the leaders' robes, the sequined shawls, or *palla*, of the women, the simple white and dusty tan tunics of the commoners, and the azure blue of the sky above. She thought she could even hear the sounds of the Imperial City, the knock-knock of wooden-wheeled carts as they clattered over cobblestoned streets, the tapping of a prelate's staff as he tried to call the gathered crowd to silence, and the orations of magistrates standing on the steps of the temples.

Giorgio let her mind conjure these images, then he returned to his own lecture.

"The land itself was either a swamp, according to some historians, or an ancient Etruscan burial ground." Shaking his head, he added, "I cannot understand why someone with great ambition would choose a swamp upon which to build their city."

"But the early Americans chose to build their capital, Washington, D.C., in what was once a swamp," Tamara offered.

Giorgio shook his head again.

"*Sì*, this is true," and with a chuckle, "maybe their fates will be the same."

La Fontana di Trevi, Rome

March 1985

The days continued like this, Giorgio doing his best impression of a tour guide as Tamara listened with interest, her hand looped through the crook in his arm. They shared meals, walked the ancient streets, and gazed at the illuminated beauty of Rome at night.

They chose a new piazza each evening, and twice ended up on the rooftop terrace at Tamara's hotel. It stood on a rise on the Via Veneto and offered a commanding view of city, so sipping the fine wines from the Enoteca Buccone was an obvious, and welcome, treat.

It took several days for Giorgio to ask Tamara about her schedule, and when she had planned to leave. She lied. Her flight home had been scheduled for two days prior, and she changed it so that she could remain in Rome with Giorgio. But, this time, she simply answered, "tomorrow." She hid the fact that she had delayed departure already but, still, saying "tomorrow" nearly brought tears to her eyes.

Giorgio gave a hint that he knew the truth, mostly through the intense look in his eyes. But he didn't dispute it.

"And you will be coming back?"

Tamara shrugged a little, but tightened her grip on his arm.

"Of course," she said, looking down at first, then glancing up at Giorgio.

They went to the Trevi Fountain, *La Fontana di Trevi,* on their last evening together.

"It's named after a young man who, when his lover was slain by a wild animal, cast himself into the Tiber to drown," said Giorgio.

"Wow! How romantic."

But Giorgio only laughed and replied, "Well, no, it's not, but I think that story is better than the truth."

"Then what's the truth?"

"This is the Trevi district of Rome. It's just a neighborhood."

"Huh," Tamara huffed. "You're right, your story is better."

Twilight had passed and, when the sky darkened, the lights that illuminated the fountain came alive.

"It's beautiful, no?" Giorgio said, staring up at Nicola Salvi's magical creation. "But it's an architect's nightmare."

"What? Why?"

He transferred the almond biscotti to his left hand and pointed with his right. "There is a building behind it. Buildings must have doors, and windows, and...well, things."

"That sounds very un-architect like," Tamara declared with a laugh. "Things? What are things?"

"The things that give a building its life. The gargoyles, the columns, the sculpted cherubs... those things."

Giorgio always had a playful way of phrasing things, but this seemed very unusual. Then Tamara realized the Giorgio was playing her. The twinkle in his eye gave him away, and she jabbed him in the arm, once, then again, a playful strike. Warning him not to mock her.

"I read that tourists throw about 3,000 euros every day into that fountain, more than Pope Clement paid to have it constructed in the 1700s," he said.

"Why do people throw money in the fountain?"

"They make a wish and they think their wish will be granted because they make an offering, a sacrifice, to whatever god or gods are listening. And for all those tourists who come to Rome, the wish is the same, no?"

"Let me guess," she replied. "They are wishing to return to Rome someday."

Giorgio nodded and smiled.

Tamara faced Giorgio and turned her back to the fountain, then threw a handful of coins over her shoulder and into the air. Hearing them splash into the water, she thought that she had sealed her future.

Dinner with Julie

March 2017

"You said you saw Giorgio again, another few times?" she asked.

I explained to Julie that when I was leaving Rome that time, I agreed to come back to see him again. He was going to be traveling for a while, and I had to get back to my job anyway. So, I couldn't just quit everything and stay.

That part of the explanation seemed easy for me to tell, but as I said the words so casually I could tell that Julie was suddenly becoming aware of how serious was my relationship with Giorgio.

"You weren't really just going to chuck it all and stay, were you?" Julie's words carried a degree of uncertainty, as if she were discovering a part of her mother she had never known.

I didn't answer; I didn't shake my head, and her eyebrows pinched together for a moment, then relaxed.

"You went back. When?"

"It was in September that year, six months later."

"Were you alone?"

"No." But then I wondered whether Julie meant did I travel alone or did I, in fact, find Giorgio.

"No, I wasn't alone. Giorgio and I planned to spend time together."

That was that. Julie didn't need to hear all the details. She could figure out that her mother, thirty-two at the time, single and smitten with a guy in Rome, wasn't going to be spending her nights alone.

"He met me at the airport and..." I paused because I couldn't stifle the giggle. "He said we were going straight to a restaurant. No stopping at the hotel to drop my bags or freshen up. 'You don't need to be any fresher,' he said. Straight to a restaurant. 'It's midday,' he said. 'You have to eat.' "

"Actually, though, we didn't go straight to a restaurant."

I paused a half second too long and Julie's eyes darkened, then she looked down at her plate. I had to reassure her for the moment.

"The airport is outside of town and he pulled his Fiat into traffic and began a long, circuitous tour of the environs around Rome. We were spiraling toward the center of the city, a drive Giorgio called *un cavatappo*, a corkscrew, so I could see the sites from outside the city inward. It was quite nice, too. In my several trips to Rome, I had always taken the train from the airport, or a taxi directly in, and my memory of sites were always those in the city itself. But the land outside of Rome was worth seeing too. I had just never done it before."

"Did you ever get to have lunch?"

"Oh, yeah," I said for emphasis. "Giorgio said I probably didn't eat well on the plane – which I hadn't – but I couldn't help but think that he meant I hadn't eaten well since I left Italy six months before. 'I have to make that up to you,' he said."

By that time, Julie and I had finished our dinner, even as slowly as I was eating. She stood to clear the plates while I sat alone with my thoughts.

I heard a little clatter of dishes in the next room, and Julie walked through the dining area into another room on the side. In a few minutes, she returned carrying a bottle of red wine. She set it down gently on the table and brandished a corkscrew.

"This is a good wine," she said, "not a great wine, but it seems like the perfect thing for us to share right now."

Julie expertly opened the bottle, not as easily or quickly as the waiters in Rome, but displaying an comfortable familiarity with the device. Then she turned to the cabinet inside the kitchen, produced two stemmed wine glasses, and returned to the table. She poured an ample serving in each glass, and slid one across to me.

"Tell me more," Julie said, as if I was one of her college peers sharing stories of a recent vacation.

Postelletti's, Rome

September 1985

They reached a point near the center of the city, or so it seemed from the crowds, the noise, and the kamikaze cab drivers angling their taxis between and among the pedestrian steams crossing the streets. It was just past midday in the middle of the work week, and the throngs had not yet been whittled down to a manageable mass. But they all seemed intent on getting somewhere, and Giorgio tapped patiently on the wheel with his left index finger as he gestured with his right hand, reminding Tamara of the pulsing beat of the city.

"Oh, yes, I know, it's busy," he explained, "but so is New York, no?"

Before Tamara could get out a cogent reply, he continued.

"But New York, it also has a rhythm!"

Tamara glanced out the window of his Fiat and took in the familiarity of the streets, the cars, the sounds, and the people that represented what Giorgio called the pulsing beat of Rome. And she smiled.

"What about Baltimore?" he asked.

"Nice. It has its own personality, but it's not Roma," she replied.

"Chicago?"

"Too hectic. Some culture, but not mine," Tamara said.

"Dallas?"

Tamara couldn't even figure out why Giorgio inquired about that southern metropolis, but in her best Italian, she said merely, "*beh*," to indicate too little interest for her to register a reply.

"Oh, but San Francisco!" Giorgio pressed.

Here, Tamara had to stop and smile back at him, her eyebrows raised in obvious approbation.

"San Francisco is the most beautiful city in America," she opined, "perhaps as beautiful as Florence."

She knew that challenging Giorgio's home for top honors would be met with a retort, but it didn't come. Giorgio nodded, his lips pursed together in a look that combined concentration and agreement, and simply said, "*è vero*" – it's true.

The car creeped forward past one traffic light only to be stuck in a column of cars lined up behind the next one. Giorgio pressed his left foot down on the clutch pedal and his right on the brake, slowing the Fiat easily and stopping just inches behind the auto in front of them. Turning to Tamara, he continued his review of American cities.

"And what of your city, Washington, D.C.?"

"It's gorgeous," she responded with sincerity. "There are wide avenues, little squares of green parks dotting the boulevards, bigger-than-life sculptures of great Americans, and low buildings never any more than several stories high. The affect is to open the city to the sky so that you're not living in a concrete canyon between towering glass and steel monstrosities."

"Sounds like you were praising D.C. while disparaging New York, all in one sentence," he said with a grin.

Tamara just gave a little shrug and a slight smile.

After another half hour, they reached Postelletti's, a cozy trattoria near the Piazza Venezia. Finding a place to leave the car would be a problem, so Giorgio offered to let Tamara out at the door and return to find her.

"No way," she protested. "I'll stay with you."

He pulled the car around the corner, stopped in a little alley and put the Fiat in park. Stepping out of the car, he tossed his keys to a young man in blue jeans and short-sleeved checkered shirt.

"*Roberto, per favore…*" he called out.

"Ah, so I see that parking the car was not as hard as you said it would be," Tamara chided him.

Giorgio raised an eyebrow and threw his hands up.

"Of course, it would have been if you had not been with me."

They walked around the corner and entered through the heavy oaken door that had "Postelletti's" inscribed on it in cursive. The sounds of the street faded behind them as they entered the darkened room of the restaurant, but those sounds were replaced by another set of noises. Inside, it was the cacophony of mixed conversations that filled the room, chirped out to the beat of knives and forks striking the plates and wine glasses thudding down on the tables. Postelletti's was not overly loud, but in the true fashion of an Italian dining room, it wasn't quiet either.

Giorgio and Tamara slipped into a booth just inside the front door and took the menus handed to them by the man who had directed them to the table.

"Prosecco," Giorgio said. "LaMarca."

Tamara recalled that sparkling wine, from their lunch at Ristorante Farini in March, and suddenly the jet lag melted away and she felt like she was back in familiar surroundings. No, it was more than that. She felt like she had returned to the place she was meant to be.

The waiter soon returned with the bottle and two glasses. As he worked the foil off the top of the bottle and eased the mushroom-shaped cork out, Giorgio pointed a finger in the air.

"*Fiori di zucca*," he requested. He then turned to Tamara and explained.

"It's zucchini blossoms stuffed with mozzarella, breadcrumbs, and anchovies, then fried. Gets your appetite going."

The plate of *fiori di zucca* arrived alongside another dish Giorgio hadn't mentioned.

"Ah, *pandorato*!" he exclaimed, but threw a quizzical look toward the waiter, as if to ask why this was delivered.

The man was busy filling their glasses with bubbly, so without pausing he merely jerked his head to the side to indicate a table across the dining room. Giorgio looked over and recognized a smiling woman waving back at him. At first, Tamara remained still and quiet, not knowing the best way to handle this, but Giorgio broke the silence.

"A happy customer," he said, and Tamara decided to let that mean an architectural customer.

Giorgio lifted the platter of *pandorato* and offered some to Tamara.

"It's a little sandwich of bread, filled with prosciutto and mozzarella, that they flour and fry in the pan."

The effervescence of the Prosecco turned out to be the perfect foil for these two fried appetizers.

Giorgio reached out to take Tamara's hand.

"I'm so glad you've come back."

He wanted to add more, but the right words didn't reach his lips. Tamara smiled back and nodded agreement.

"I enjoyed my last trip so much," she added, "but it wasn't just the city, you know."

The meal passed with them catching up on what they had been doing for the last six months. New plates of food arrived – including *carbonara* for Giorgio and *fettucine alla papalina* for Tamara. His was a very traditional dish from central Italy, thin noodles tossed with savory prosciutto, chunks of mild sausage, diced sautéed onion, parsley, egg, and Parmesan cheese. Tamara's was also a pasta dish – excellent pairings for the Prosecco Giorgio had ordered – dressed with Parmesan, butter, peas, and ham.

When the plates were cleared, Giorgio relaxed with his last glass of Prosecco but gently pressed Tamara to order the *tiramisu.*

"Rome's best!" he insisted, and she relented. During her months back in the States, Tamara recalled the many Italian dishes she had discovered with Giorgio, but sitting now at one of these restaurants, she was reminded of the stamina she needed to complete a full meal.

"After this," Giorgio told her, "I'll drop you at your hotel."

The jet lag that had been held in abeyance was slowing creeping up on Tamara. Her eyelids were lowered to half-mast – a clue that Giorgio might have picked up on – and her ability to stifle the yawns was waning.

So, after paying the check, Giorgio did as he promised. He helped Tamara up to her room, carrying her suitcase so that she could lean on the stairway railing for support – either from exhaustion or wine – then handed her the key and departed.

Dinner with Julie

March 2017

"It was the scent of the city," I said suddenly. It was an abrupt realization, but it occurred to me that Rome, like most cities, has a certain aroma. It's not just the food I had been enjoying. It was the fragrance of fresh flowers at the kiosk just outside my hotel, the heady aroma of roasted coffee beans from the espresso bars that crowded every block of the city. It was the perfume of fresh pastries in the morning, sauced pastas and broiled meat during the day, the heavenly aroma of sausages grilling on the outdoor restaurant patios, the trace elements of wine that filled every dining room.

It was even the odor of car exhaust and cigarette smoke. Everything mixed into a fantastic symphony for the nose.

And when I returned to be with Giorgio, I rediscovered that symphony, and I realized how important it was to me, and how I had longed to come back.

But when I spoke that brief sentence out loud to Julie, it didn't have all the details that filled my brain.

"Yes, I know, mom," Julie replied.

My daughter had traveled some, too, and she probably understood the basics of my terse declaration. But it would have been tedious for me to repeat all the senses to convince her of how the smells of Rome had affected me.

Julie poured some more wine for each of us and I continued my description of Rome, of Giorgio, and of me.

Altare della Patria, Rome

September 1985

That evening, after Tamara had enjoyed a restorative nap, they walked together back toward Piazza Venezia. It was one of the hubs of Rome, and in the middle of the large open space towered the Altare della Patria, what many tourists called "the wedding cake" because of its symmetrical wings, gleaming white façade, and layered stacks of marble.

"This," Giorgio said pointing to the massive structure, "was built in honor of Vittorio Emanuele II, the first king of a united Italy. Many people think that Italy has been a country for thousands of years, but not so!" he added with emphasis on the word. "We were many countries…"

"Until 1860," Tamara interrupted.

Giorgio smiled, nodding his head in approbation.

"How did you discover this?" he asked her.

Tamara had a fair understanding of Roman history, but hadn't discovered this fact until she returned from Rome six months earlier, and decided to brush up on the subject. But she was not going to let Giorgio know this. His Italian pride would insist on taking credit for inspiring her.

The sun was still high in the sky, but the temperature was pleasant and a whiff of a fresh breeze stirred occasionally. They walked along arm in arm, talking about things they had done in the preceding six months and what plans Giorgio had made for them now that Tamara had returned to Rome.

She spoke of her work and the frustrating clients she dealt with occasionally. Giorgio was typically more reserved about his work, something that Tamara had noticed on her last visit but not something she thought much about. Architecture seemed like a more interesting career than her own as an accountant, but Giorgio always appeared more interested in talking about her, or Rome, and of course food.

They worked their way up the Via del Corso, then turned right along Via dell'Umiltà. Tamara recognized it as heading in the direction of the Trevi Fountain, and the thought brought a smile to her face. But Giorgio passed by the little side street they had taken on Tamara's last night in Rome back in March, and turned left, right, and then left again, almost a meandering route that she now understood to be Giorgio's way of absorbing the essence of what is Rome.

Before long, they arrived at the foot of the Spanish Steps. While Tamara gazed in awe at the famous *scalinata,* Giorgio continued his non-stop chatter about Roman history and art. With her attention averted to the steps, Giorgio finally recognized that Tamara was distracted, so he broke off his narrative.

"Ah, *sì, La Scalinata di Spagna,*" he said with some reverence. "The stairway to heaven."

Tamara shot him a curious look, wondering what this wondrous place had to do with heaven, or with the American song by the same name. Knowing that he had left her without words, Giorgio rested his left hand on her arm, and pointed with his right toward the church at the top.

"*Santissima Trinità dei Monti,* the Most Holy Trinity of the Mountain."

Tamara raised her chin to look up to the top of the Spanish Steps, toward the church edifice at the summit, an Italian Renaissance building whose prominent position at the top of these steps certainly gave the impression of a gateway to heaven.

"But there are more important churches in Rome," she said, and Giorgio agreed.

"St. Peter's among them," Tamara noted, and added, "and Basilica di San Pietro in Vincoli," easily recalling the church Giorgio had introduced her to on her last Roman holiday.

Tamara took in the panorama of it all. Standing at the bottom of the Steps, with the Piazza di Spagna behind her, and in the center of the piazza the grand *Fontana della Barcaccia,* she looked heavenward toward the white obelisk on the plateau of the church framed by the white face of *Trinità dei Monti* at the crest.

Without any warning, Giorgio plopped down on the steps. Tamara looked down at him for a moment grinning and impressed with his impulsiveness. The man always seemed to possess the city, not just inhabit it, she thought, as she sat down beside him.

They remained silent for some time, until Giorgio turned toward her.

"What would you do with your life? No...different question," he revised. "What would you want to do with your life?"

It was an interesting query, and Tamara reflected for a moment on the difference between the two questions. She might know what she would do with her life, although quietly acknowledged to herself that she didn't have any clue. But what would she *want* to do with her life? That was both a bigger question and an easier one to answer.

"I'd stay here with you," she said finally, then her eyes opened wide with the realization of what she had said so impulsively.

Giorgio didn't smile, as she had expected him to do. He didn't acknowledge the obvious compliment, but he also didn't seem put off by the idea. He just looked at Tamara, then cast his gaze downward in a show of shyness she wasn't used to from this man.

"So would I," he said after a moment.

Tamara was sitting on the step above him, but leaned down and kissed Giorgio softly. They both welcomed the touch in a way that was clearly warmer and more intense than any kiss that preceded it. Their relationship, which had been one of pleasure and happiness, had taken a sudden turn toward romance. The newness of this registered in their faces – and in Tamara's nervous giggle when their lips parted – but it also registered deeper in their souls.

Il Teatro Ristorante, Rome

September 1985

"Food is a performance here," Giorgio said. "And, so, they call it 'The Theatre.' "

The weather was still mild and Giorgio requested a table out on the terrace. He and Tamara sat down in a position to enjoy the grand fountain in the piazza across from the restaurant. There were tourists aplenty, and pigeons to outnumber them, but the elevated platform that the restaurant used for its outdoor tables kept their clients raised a few feet above the crowd. There was only the din of pedestrian traffic and the occasional car horn; but otherwise it seemed like a private balcony.

Menus were delivered and the waiter poured sparkling water into sturdy tumblers on the table. Giorgio wasted no time ordering two glasses of Prosecco.

"Yum," Tamara chimed in.

Giorgio sat back in his chair and allowed a stern look to cast a shadow on his face.

"You found Prosecco in Rome, with me," and then the suspicious grin. "Have you been having Prosecco with someone else?"

His playful repartee only barely hid a subtle insecurity. Sure, Tamara had first discovered Prosecco with his help, but she had spent those long months back in the States. He doubted that she was alone when not with him.

"Yes," she responded gaily, but then lowered her eyes. She reached across and rested her hand on his, and said, "No, Giorgio. No."

Without very many words, they seemed to have crossed a bridge together. Both were alone during the six months since Tamara's last visit, and it was clear then that both had chosen to wait for their reunion to see what life held for them.

And both seemed to conclude that it was worth the wait.

A waiter abruptly interrupted their interlude to pass out menus and Giorgio and Tamara assumed a more serious position. Just as the waiter was about to spin on his heel and depart, Giorgio raised his index finger.

"*E con la cibo, due bicchieri di vino bianco di casa,*" he said to the man – "and with the meal, two glasses of the house white wine. Tamara could translate this easily and was surprised that Giorgio would settle for house wine.

"Ah, *beh,*" he said with upturned palms. "It is the wine of my cousin, in Lombardy."

Tamara smiled, shaking her head at how connected her companion was with Rome, with Italy, and with the regions around it.

"I noticed that you didn't order a nice little French wine," she teased, knowing full well that Il Teatro would not stock such wines.

"French? The French make wine?" he replied. "That's so wonderful, I should try some sometime."

"So," he continued, "you didn't answer my question. What would you do with your life?"

"Oh, but I did," she replied, eyes lowered slightly, as in to hide a shy side that wasn't often revealed.

"*Sì, sì,* I know," he said. But then he slid his hands around her right hand, pressed gently but firmly, and continued.

"You have brought life into my life," then he stopped to think about his words. "But I may not be for you."

This was the first time that Tamara had even thought that this romance might not work out. She wondered whether he was simply demurring, or whether Giorgio had introduced doubts that she didn't have.

The Prosecco was gone and the waiter returned with two glasses of white wine, the bowl of each glistening with the light condensation on the glass. Tamara touched hers and a tear shimmered at the edge of her eye. But she tried to shake off the thought, at least for a moment.

"Here's to finding out," she toasted, lifting the glass to Giorgio. He copied her action and smiled back at her. Noticing the moisture in her eyes, he tried to recover.

"I want you, Tamara, and we are together. Yes, I doubt sometimes why you would spend time with me, but let's not think about that. It's maybe just my insecurity in the company of someone as wonderful as you."

His speech did little to settle Tamara's concerns. She wasn't sure whether Giorgio's reticence was a true impediment to their relationship, or whether there was another undisclosed problem.

After a sip of wine and a moment to sit, they regathered their thoughts and turned their attention back to the menu.

"*Minestra alla viterbese*," Tamara said to the waiter, a soup rich in pureed vegetables and semolina. "*Allora, saltimbocca alla romana*," she added, folding her menu and handing it back to the waiter, asking for chicken breast with a thin slice of prosciutto and layer of melted cheese.

"*Bazzoffia*," Giorgio added, requesting a soup of fava beans, peas, and artichokes, "*e spaghetti a cacio e pepe*," a simple dish of pasta with grated parmesan and pepper.

Their first courses soon arrived and they sat in relative quiet for a while, both of them a bit on edge about how to continue. Tamara didn't want to ask Giorgio why he wouldn't be good for her, but she needed an opening. Something to break the ice and return their evening to open conversation.

"Are you married?" Again, Tamara surprised herself by blurting out the question.

"*No, mi amore.* I'm not married." Giorgio sensed that the dinner was going off the rails and that his comment had caused it.

"I am not married. Of course, I would not be here with you if I was."

"But why aren't you the right man for me?"

Giorgio sensed an opening and took it.

"I didn't say I wasn't, only that I might not be. My work, well, I travel and that's not fair to you."

"You should let me decide that," she protested. In the shadow of the subtle comment that led up to this, both Giorgio and Tamara realized that they were venturing into a discussion deeper, and with more commitment, than before.

"I am quite capable of deciding what I do with my life," she continued. It was a terse and forceful comment, as much to push back on Giorgio's reservations as to point out to him that she would not be denied the freedom to make her own choices.

Giorgio lowered his head and she could see him lightly nodding, as his chin tapped near his chest in agreement with her.

"*Mi dispiace*," he said – "I'm sorry" – then looking back up at her, added, "I am a proud Roman," and Tamara immediately wondered why he said Roman and not Tuscan. But Giorgio pressed on.

"I take you around my city and show off the wonders of Rome…" Again, she wondered why he was pressing Rome into his biography.

"And I entertain you with these wonderful meals and wondrous wines. But I don't want to disappoint you."

"Why do you think you would disappoint me?"

Giorgio chose that moment to switch the tone, lighten their talk, and he smiled broadly back at Tamara.

"I don't think so, and I don't want to," and he was saved by the return of the waiter.

"Pio Cesare Barolo," he said to the man. Tamara had also secretly been researching Italian wines while back at home, and she knew enough about it that Barolo stood out as a singular wine. She wasn't familiar with the producer, but looked forward to another long, languishing dinner to accompany it.

The waiter returned with a basket of bread, including *grissini, bigne* – a type of flower-shaped bread unique to Rome – and glistening squares of *focaccia* redolent of oregano, red pepper flakes and olive oil. He displayed the bottle of wine for approval, but Giorgio quickly pointed to Tamara for the taste, surprising both her and the waiter.

"You've been studying," he leaned in close to tell her. "I can tell from your comments about wine in general. Besides, it's the 21st century even in Italy!"

The waiter circled the table and approached Tamara, pouring a little sample into her glass. The man then stood up straight and about a foot back from the table. Giorgio looked up at his face and couldn't quite tell whether the waiter was amused or concerned at this modernized ritual.

Lifting the glass and giving it a practiced swirl, Tamara sniffed – eyebrows raised – and drew a bit into her mouth.

"Supple. Reminds me of crushed berries with a whiff of tobacco leaf and herbs," she said, and then paused. "Very good!"

The waiter looked surprised but pleased, and nodded both to Tamara and to Giorgio in a professional, polished way.

"*È vero*," he pronounced – "it's true" – and resumed his task of filling their glasses with the deep ruby red wine.

For the rest of the evening, they avoided difficult subjects. Tamara hid her concern, but Giorgio noticed it. At the end of the meal, over espresso and little *giglietti* cookies, he ventured back to their earlier conversation.

"I spoiled the evening," he began, but Tamara shook her head "no."

"Yes, I was too reserved when you told me how you felt. I've never been this way before. The women in my life were mostly entertaining and sometimes serious, but I wasn't. I guess I don't know how to deal with this."

"Should I go back to America?"

"Oh, please no," he said gripping her hand. "That's not what I want." Smiling broadly, Giorgio concluded, "If you'll be patient… " but he let the sentence drop.

Dinner with Julie

March 2017

Julie was still looking at me, but I sensed that she had many thoughts running through her head. She was digesting my tale of romance, and trying to figure Giorgio out from a distance of time and space, trying to do something that was difficult for me even when I sat across the table from him.

"That wasn't your last night in Rome, was it?"

"No, honey. I was staying for three more days."

"Did you talk more about that?"

"Yes, and no. We talked more about serious topics, but we still enjoyed the fun times and lights and liveliness of Rome together."

"What serious topics?"

I paused a beat too long.

"What serious topics, mom?"

"Whether – no when – we should get married."

Campo de' Fiori, Rome

September 1985

The sunny skies and moderate temperature made the following day perfect for walking. Giorgio and Tamara woke early and remained in bed with just a single sheet to ward off the morning breeze that occasionally swept in through the open window.

"I must go get ready," Giorgio said, rising suddenly from the bed and retrieving his clothes. They were spending nights together by then, but he didn't move into her hotel suite, so he spent the first part of every morning returning to his own home to shower and dress.

Tamara had already suggested that they stay at his place. She could bring her suitcase along and he would be already in his place.

"That's perfect," Giorgio replied, pulling the belt buckle closed on his pants and slipping his sock-less feet into his leather loafers. "We'll do that."

But Tamara had already unpacked into her room and they had already established a routine, so he suggested, "The next time, we will start out that way, and you don't have to reserve a hotel room."

"The next time?" Tamara asked, teasing him but also venturing into the future of her imagining.

"*Sì*, there will be a next time, and another, and another," he assured her.

After Giorgio pulled the door closed behind him, Tamara stretched her arms in a show of sheer happiness and relief. When her arms rested back on the sheet, her mind wandered back to the night before and the inscrutable conversation they had had. They both seemed to realize that there was a new, though hopefully small tension, but neither wanted to address it outright and force the tension into the open.

"He should have more confidence," Tamara announced to no one in particular, raising her arms again in a stretch, content to dispense with the subject without investigating it.

She tossed the sheet off and rose to shower and prepare for another day with Giorgio.

* * *

By late morning, they were in *Campo de' Fiori*, a little neighborhood known for its market in summer, and for its central location year-round.

"Most tourists don't discover this little treasure until their second trip to Rome," Giorgio pointed out.

"Well, this is my fifth trip to Rome, and I've never been here, to this square," quipped Tamara.

"And I am pleased to introduce you to it," he replied, squeezing her arm. "It dates back to ancient Rome, but then it was just a field."

"Campo means field, right?" she asked.

"*Sì*," he said, but before he could complete the thought, Tamara chimed in.

"And *fiori* is flowers."

"Ah, you know this," Giorgio commented with pleasure.

"Of course. Like I told you, don't underestimate me."

He then pointed to the church on the perimeter and to the large hooded statue in the center of the piazza.

"He must have been famous," Tamara opined, but Giorgio only laughed.

"Yes, famous. That's Giordano Bruno. In 1600, he was burned at the stake, right there," he said, pointing to the foot of the platform that held the statue. "For heresy."

"Wait," she objected. "Italians put a statue of someone executed for heresy in this square?"

"*Sì*, well, it's complicated," he offered. "His writings were relegated to the *Index Librorum Prohibitorum.* That's Latin for..."

"Index of Forbidden Books," she interjected. "I know of it. The index was the Catholic Church's list of books their faithful were not allowed to read. But that's medieval."

"*Sì,* but as I said, that was in 1600."

"Still," Tamara pressed. "Why a statue to him?"

At this Giorgio let out a little chuckle.

"Italy is entitled to its opinions, and so is the Church. And opinions can change. Ettore Ferrari, a sculptor from the 1800s, didn't like what had happened to Bruno. So, he carved this beautiful statue and placed it right here, over the proverbial ashes, and he turned the statue to face – no, stare directly at – the Vatican."

Tamara squinted at the inscription at the base of the statue, and struggled momentarily to translate it.

" 'To Bruno – the century predicted by him – here where the fire burned,' " she was able to tease out.

"He was a Dominican friar, but among other talents," Giorgio said, "Bruno was a student of the heavens, of astronomy and cosmology. He was declared a heretic because he subscribed to the Copernican model of the universe; he even postulated that life might exist on other planets. For that, he was executed by the church."

"And by the 19th century," Tamara concluded, "both science and religion had come to agree that the sun is just a star, and our planet revolves around it, not the other way around."

"*Giusto*" – "just that" – said Giorgio. "And he was – what do Americans say? – rehabilitated?"

The rest of the morning they spent wandering among the tents and booths of the market, and Tamara marveled at the freshness and aroma of the fruits and vegetables displayed in the open air. Along the perimeter of the square, they stopped for coffee, espresso for Giorgio and cappuccino for Tamara, sipping at their drinks from the counter that surrounded the establishment's outdoor façade.

As noon approached, the crowds loosened and Giorgio and Tamara went on their way, in search of a restaurant for *pranzo.*

The Capitoline Hill, Rome

September 1985

Giorgio and Tamara worked their way along the busy streets of Rome on this, a workday, but found some quiet time on the Capitoline Hill, one of the seven hills upon which ancient Rome was founded.

"The Capitoline Hill refers to *Capitolium*, another word for temple," Giorgio explained. "The Romans thought that such a temple was indestructible, and so it represented eternity."

"Hence, the Eternal City," suggested Tamara.

"Exactly."

"The architecture is spectacular here, and the sculptures!"

"The plateau, just here," he said pointing to the flat area atop the steps and sandwiched between the towering equestrian statues, "is called the *Piazza del Campidoglio*, and it was designed by Michelangelo. These are government buildings," Giorgio explained.

"This is such magnificent architecture," Tamara said. "Have you anything quite like this to claim as your own?" she said, teasing Giorgio.

He looked at her squarely, with the one side of his mouth trying to smile, but with a gray cast that shrouded his eyes' usual sparkle. Giorgio was trying to speak but could not find the right words.

Tamara noticed the pause and wondered once again where her words had taken them.

"Tell me about your buildings, what do you like best?" she asked, shifting the subject to more solid ground.

Again, Giorgio paused but the smile won the battle for his face.

"Mostly office buildings, and some schools," he said.

"Are they here, in Rome?"

"Yes, but all over," he responded. His arm waved in that general way he did when they first met and he was showing Tamara where his office was.

"What made you choose architecture? Tell me what you like most about it," she asked.

For this, there was no hesitation in his voice.

"I like to have an idea, a picture in my mind, to imagine the vertical lines of the structure emerging from the ground to meet intersecting lines, both horizontal and slanted. I can close my eyes and see inside that structure," and here he did close his eyes, "the rooms and hallways, even the people moving around inside it.

"There are arches...there will always be arches."

"Why?" Tamara was amused by this firm statement.

"People don't realize that there are many arches, as many as there are windows or doors or other openings. There's the Roman, or round arch..."

"But of course," Tamara interjected, smiling, but Giorgio continued.

"The lancet arch, segmental arch, inverse or inflex arch, the horseshoe arch, Tudor, parabolic..."

"Okay, okay," she laughed. "I get it. But why the focus on arches? Is it just your fascination with the art form?"

"Yes, I've always pictured buildings according to their openings, according to the way the inside opens itself to the outside...through its arches.

"But arches also hold the building up," he continued. "They...really any opening...are the most vulnerable place in a building. Designed properly, and protected, the opening is safe. Mistakes in the design, even subtle mistakes not caught by the architect in time, and the building can come down in a heap."

Giorgio looked back up at the structures on the Capitoline Hill, and Tamara's eyes followed them. She saw the flat-top windows and doors, the arches in the clock tower and front entrance, and the ornamental pediments above each opening.

"What are those for?" she asked, pointed to the building. "The decorative things above the door. Pediments, right?"

"Yes, but as you said, they're merely decorative. The weight of the building is not supported by them. that's the job of the arch."

He studied the formation of the piazza and the buildings upon the rise, quiet for a moment while he took it all in.

"Stunning, isn't it," Tamara said to pull Giorgio out of his reverie. He nodded, but continued studying the architecture.

Piazza della Rotonda, Pantheon, Rome

September 1985

"I think we should find someplace for lunch." Tamara said this as they returned to their meandering walk around the city. Giorgio was pensive since they left the *Campidoglio* and she wondered what he was thinking. Food usually brought him back to the present. And it worked this time too.

They were on a narrow, cobbled street where two-way traffic fought for space to pass the oncoming cars. The sidewalks were also narrow, so pedestrians became combatants in the struggle, stepping up on the raised stone at times, or stepping down off the sidewalk to circle around a planter or shop display that jutted out onto the walkway. It was slow going with a frequent brush with a passing car, and Giorgio and Tamara held hands to squeeze between the lines of traffic.

The buildings on this street were only a few stories high, but the slender street meant that only a sliver of sky was visible above. And the stone fronts of the adjoining buildings took on the appearance of a canyon wall.

Suddenly, at one intersection, the line of walls on the street fell away and opened onto a large semi-circular piazza cluttered with tables and tourists jostling with the metal chairs and one another. The sky opened up too, and filled the vast opening above them, as Tamara looked to her left and saw the magnificent rise of the Pantheon, its massive pillars and imposing domed roof dominating the square. She had seen the structure before, been inside, and even sat at the tables in the piazza for coffee or wine, but this time she was stunned by the suddenness of it all.

"I know the Pantheon from past visits, but wandering the streets like we did, I had no idea we were near it. This is such a glorious structure; in America, it would be set out in an open field with long avenues of approach to allow sightseers to gaze at it from the distance."

"Rome doesn't have open fields and long avenues of approach," chuckled Giorgio. "The city is thousands of years old, and it has been a crowded city forever."

"Of course, I know that. But the suddenness of it all, to be walking down a street and literally bump into one of the greatest structures in the world, a ruin that's been here for...what...two thousand years?"

"Yes, exactly. It was built by Marcus Agrippa," he added, "see here." Then he pointed to the Latin inscription over the pillars.

"But it's not a ruin. It was a temple in Agrippa's time, well, a private one for his use alone. Over the centuries it has been burned, torn down, and rebuilt."

"Kings are buried there, right?" asked Tamara.

"Yes, Vittorio Emanuele II and Umberto I, plus Queen Margherita. But back to what I was saying, it's not a ruin. It is still considered a church by the Roman Catholics."

"Are there services there?"

"Not the common liturgy," he indicated, but winked when he added, "but some Romans say there are pagan practices that take place at night."

Tamara's sideways glance told him she didn't buy that story.

"Then there would be witnesses," she declared with confidence.

"Not if the pagan practices involved only spirits," Giorgio added with another wink.

"Is this where we're having lunch?" Tamara asked.

"Oh, no," Giorgio said, wagging his finger. "These cafés are for tourists," and he led her across the piazza to another street that gave them an escape from the throngs of people.

"Rome wasn't built in a day," he said, making Tamara chuckle.

"Where did that come from?"

"I think Americans use that to say, 'things take time,' right?" he asked.

She nodded yes, but still didn't follow.

"Well, we say it too," Giorgio continued. "But we mean it in a different way. 'Rome wasn't built in a day' refers to how the houses and buildings were thrown up beside winding pathways that later became streets. How the streets themselves were dirt paths meant for barefooted peasants, and later set with cobblestones, first for horse-drawn wagons and pushcarts, and only later paved for automobiles that have tried with difficulty to snake through them ever since. How windows were cut into the sides of buildings overlooking open spaces without planning that those open spaces would one day be blocked by another building – with windows carved into the sides and looking back at you.

"Rome is a very old city that was not very planned, but grew up organically. Oh, don't get me wrong, this is one of the traits that Romans like about their home. But the winding streets, clusters of buildings, cafés squeezed into alleys between storefronts, these things make tourists roll their eyes."

They continued talking about the city's idiosyncrasies while stepping between the throngs of people walking toward, or away from the Pantheon. Store owners waved and called out to their neighbors, a huge espresso machine hissed steam out an open window, cups and saucers clattered while workers tossed back their java for the day, and compact cars slogged along through the crowds trying to reach the next intersection, only to find another crowd of pedestrians in their way.

Tamara thought how sometimes people say that this thing or that thing take on a life of their own. And how Giorgio's description of Rome – and the sights and sounds around her – were evidence of that here in the Eternal City. But this time the phrase became ever truer for her.

Alberto's Trattoria, Rome

September 1985

"*Qui*," the waiter said, "here," pointing to the table just inside the dining room.

Giorgio and Tamara sat as instructed, choosing two seats beside each other and with their backs to the wall, the better to see the other people in the dining room. Tamara naturally took such seats as she liked to people-watch when she was in a restaurant. Giorgio was trained by Italian custom to do the same, but for a different reason. He joked that no Italian man wanted to have his back to the open room, as if this was somehow dangerous.

"You don't think there will be trouble, do you?" teased Tamara. Giorgio grinned at her comment but remained quite serious about his reasoning.

Menus were quickly distributed and they scanned the options to find something for their midday meal. Tamara ordered *insalata misto*, a simple tossed salad, and *mazzancolle al coccio*, shrimp cooked in olive oil, garlic, and white wine, accented with lemon rind and white pepper. Handing his menu back to the waiter, Giorgio said, "*la stessa insalata*" – "the same salad" – and "*gricia con salsiccia*" – pasta with sausage and a sauce of sautéed onions and grated cheese.

"Tell me more about your architecture," Tamara said, leaning forward to put her elbows on the table.

"I design buildings," Giorgio offered, exhibiting a reluctance to talk about himself. "I focus mostly on the structural aspects of the design; I suppose I'm not the artist." And laughing a bit, he added, "I leave the fancy stuff to others; I concern myself with whether the building will stand...or fall down."

"Is that why you seemed so engrossed by the arches we saw at the *Campidoglio* this morning?"

"Yes, I suppose. Very little is needed to hold a building upright," then gaining excitement in the subject, Giorgio began to arrange the salt and pepper shakers, water glasses, and other objects on the table. He rolled his napkin up into a tube, and did the same with Tamara's, then stood them up like columns, then tipped them toward the other so that one end of each napkin roll was on the table about six inches apart, and the other ends touched in a flat-sided triangle on the table.

"This is a pyramid, and it is very strong from the top," then gently releasing the two napkins, he let the new construction stand unaided on the table. Giorgio then picked up a knife, showed it to Tamara, and then placed it horizontally on top of the pyramid, balancing the implement carefully on the lean-to of rolled cloth. The whole thing stood, and Giorgio gave a silent gesture of victory.

"But now watch," he instructed, removing the knife and returning it to the table.

"The pyramid is an awkward structure," he said, spreading the base of the pyramid of napkins about eight inches apart. He made sure the assembly was stable, then threw a look at Tamara.

"Pyramids have narrow openings, and must be broadened to serve as doors, so we move the sides apart so people can walk through them." With this, Giorgio used his fingers to simulate a person walking through the opening in the pyramid.

"But as we open the door, we risk the stability of the pyramid."

Then he repeated his action of balancing the knife on top of the structure, causing it to fall under the weight. He looked back at Tamara with a frown.

"So, what would you do?" he tested Tamara.

She wasn't certain how to answer and thought for a moment while the wine was poured for them. They hadn't ordered any, but noting the dishes they had requested, the waiter chose an Albino Armani Pinot Grigio for the table. When he left them, Tamara had an answer.

She bent each of the tube-shaped napkin rolls into a curve, placed one end of each on the table and pointed the other ends toward each other. The construction was a pair of vertical pieces over which a bent arch met at the middle of the opening.

"*Bravo!*" said Giorgio. "*Perfetto!* This is what an arch is like." Pointing to the vertical sides, he continued, "The blocks of stone on the side are stacked up" – gently jabbing at each as if it was made of layers – "then more stones are set in a semi-circular arch on top," his fingers tracing the curve of the construction, "building slowly until they meet."

"But that's not going to work," Tamara protested. The stones at the top can't just curve. Are they cut to do that?"

"*Sì, sì*, they are cut into isosceles trapezoids…"

Tamara held up her left hand, gulping some wine with her right. "Wait, wait. Isosceles trapezoids?"

"Think of a triangle, sitting on its base, then cut off the top. You end up with a flat-top stone with a wide base and sloping sides. You cut a number of these, then flip them over." He used his hands to demonstrate the movement. "Now, assemble them so that the broad base is above and the narrower flat-top is below. With this, you create a series of stones that lean toward each other. As the sides of the arch grow toward the middle, the last stone is tapped into place. Its sideways pressure pushes against the angular stones to its left and right, and the arch stands freely!"

Giorgio gave another triumphant gesture, as if he had built an arch right before her eyes.

"It's called the Roman arch!" he added for good measure.

As if on cue, the waiter returned with their salads, then quickly departed. They both sipped from their wine glasses and lifted their forks to begin the meal, but the conversation remained on arches.

"You sound like a little boy when you talk like that," Tamara said with a smile.

"Yes, well…" Giorgio left the sentence unfinished, but he seemed to agree with her as he disassembled the napkin arch.

"The arch can hold up the entire building…or allow the entire building to come crashing down."

Before long, the waiter came to collect their small appetizer plates and replace them with the entrées. The deep savory aromas of Tamara's shrimp caught her attention before the plate was even set on the table. Giorgio's pasta was fragrant and glistened with oil. They both put aside talk of arches and architecture for a while to dive into the food.

Tamara wedged the tiny point of her knife into the shell of the shrimp, using her other hand to steady the tail and coax the meat out. The oil glistened on the crustacean and the scent of oil, lemon, and wine lifted to her nose while she waged her battle. Giorgio chuckled at her method, which seemed to work quite well for Tamara, but he reached over and snatched up one of the shrimp by the tail. Placing the meaty end between his teeth, he squeezed the shell to crack it, then he sucked out the meat with a quick draw and licked the scented oil that clung to his fingertips.

"That's all well and good for you," Tamara countered, "but my mother would be furious if I had done that in public."

"Oh, so you do that when you're alone, but not when you're in public?"

Tamara smiled.

"Well, no. I was also taught to 'practice in private what you should do in public.' "

Giorgio attacked his pasta with the same enthusiasm that he attacked Tamara's shrimp. He poked his fork into the nest of long noodles, stabbing a hunk of sausage in the process. He used the plump morsel like an anchor which held the spaghetti in place on his fork, then lifted the mouthful all in one motion. Tamara noticed that he didn't twirl the noodles like the Americans were in the habit of doing.

They ate in silence for a few moments and when the meal was reaching its end, they returned to conversation.

"Do you sit every day at your desk, pouring over people's ledgers?" Giorgio asked.

The image reminded her of a Charles Dickens' novel, with its heavy wooden furniture, dim lights, and grey cast over the scene.

"It's not like that," she said, adding "really," as if to convince herself.

"I have always loved math. I like the certainty of it, that there is only one answer for every question, and accounting is like that. The ledger must always balance, and there's only one way for that to happen."

Giorgio munched on a last bite of pasta as he considered Tamara's description of her career.

"It's rare in life to find a question that has only one answer," he said. "I envy you."

"Do you work for many people," he asked, "or are you an accountant in a firm?"

"A firm. I've been there for about six years. It's a safe, solid job, and I am well respected. I like it."

Her series of reassuring statements left Giorgio wondering whether Tamara was explaining to him or to herself how good her situation was.

"And what about you?" she countered.

Giorgio sipped some wine.

"*Sì*, of course. I like my job too," but he left it at that. "How about a walk after dinner?" Giorgio added, as if to change the subject.

Dinner with Julie

March 2017

"Mom, you and Giorgio were going to get married?"

I hadn't thought through this discussion before dinner began. And Julie's question made me realize how unprepared I was to tell her everything that was in my head. But I knew that I had come too far to turn back.

"Yes, honey, we talked about it."

"Talking about it is not the same thing as deciding to do it."

I chuckled a little, knowing that Julie was searching for more definitive answers. I looked across the table at her as she poured more wine into my glass. I could tell she was on my side, in a vague, vicarious way, and she was keeping the conversation alive by offering more wine.

I stared deeply into Julie's eyes for the first time that evening, hoping to get a clear understanding of her mood and how this news had affected her. I still worried about her thinking that this was somehow going to diminish her memory of her father, but she gazed back at me with a mixture of friendship, love, and surprise. With that signal, I concluded that the memory of Ted – and her confidence in my love for him – was secure. So I returned to my story.

"Giorgio was very easy to love."

I stopped. I thought I knew what I was going to say next, but the words wouldn't come at first.

"We decided on our last night together in Rome that I would come back again, and when I returned we would get married."

I drank a bit of wine and looked across the table at Julie. Her calm and interested look convinced me to go on, that I hadn't violated any trusts or crossed any forbidden barriers.

"He had his work, and I had mine. We still had to figure out where we would live, in Rome or the U.S. – or somewhere – but it's not like you see in the movies. That disjunction is used by script writers to doom relationships. It wasn't like that with us. Giorgio and I saw that being together would overcome that divide."

I had to laugh a little at that last part.

"He did seem a little reluctant sometimes, though," I added. "The usual 'guy-thing' about commitment, I guess. So the plan was that I would go home, work, figure out how to move this thing forward, and he would continue with his work. I would come back six months later and we'd get married."

"So…" Julie said slowly. "Mom, did you?"

I sighed, nodding at my daughter's inquisitiveness, then smiled back at her.

Mithraeum, Rome

September 1985

They left the restaurant and re-entered the light of a warm autumn afternoon in Rome. Walking arm in arm, they circled the block and meandered toward a construction site. Tamara noticed that the men and women in the pit didn't look like masonry laborers, and their tools were cleaner and smaller than the shovels and other equipment she normally saw in such places.

As they passed by the site, she glanced back at the work and could see light coming from an excavated cave at the bottom of the pit, near the bucket of a backhoe. She stopped to examine the work, and Giorgio paused with her.

"They began that work about six months ago," he said, pointing to the people bent over their labor in the hole. "When they scraped back the foundation of the old building, they found a cave below…an old cave with human remains and ceremonial pieces."

Tamara and Giorgio peered into the workspace again, and he continued.

"Rome has a long history, and many mysteries. It is said that the followers of Mithras had caves here during the time of the Roman Empire."

"I don't know Mithras," Tamara said. "What is it?"

"It came from the east, either Greece or Turkey," he replied, "possibly from Persia, ancient Iran," he added. "Mithras was a god worshiped by Romans of that day. His followers believed him to be the most powerful god, and they gathered in underground caves much like the early Christians did."

"Did they fear for their safety? That was the reason the Christians hid in catacombs."

"Yes, and no. The Mithraists were outsiders, surely, and this may have made them vulnerable to attacks from the governing elites. But they also preferred the privacy of secret places to carry out their worship practices."

"Were the ceremonies primitive, or violent?"

"Again, yes, and no. They did not practice human sacrifice, if that's what you mean. But they did have initiation rites that could be used to prove a member's loyalty to the group. And they wanted to hide these rites from outsiders to avoid infiltration by their opposition.

Most construction sites had sounds of banging and digging, but the scientists who gathered at the yawning opening of the cave below made almost no sound.

"You said Greece, right?" asked Tamara.

"*Sì*, Greece and Turkey are thought to have been the origins of the religion. But I'm sure it was old Iran."

"Why do you think that?"

"It's not just me; many Romans think that now."

"Wait, why is an ancient and mysterious religion so talked about today that you say 'many Romans?' are talking about it."

Giorgio rubbed his chin while staring down at the work below the sidewalk.

"Because there have been suspicions that some terrorists have entered Rome. And they've been spotted in several of the old Mithraic caves in its outskirts of the city."

"Why would they skulk around in caves?"

"It may not be in obeisance to Mithra," he responded. "Perhaps it's just because these caves exist and provide ready shelter for the group. Or, yes, it could have some relation to the ancient traditions of Persia...Iran."

"Sorry," Tamara added with doubt in her voice, "that doesn't make sense. Rome wouldn't want questionable characters from the Middle East in their midst, and Rome also knows where these caves are. It would be too easy to corral the infiltrators and kill or contain them."

"They don't live in the caves, but they have their gatherings there. When the Roman authorities get word of some activity at one of the caves – they're called Mithraea – they send the *polizia* to investigate, but the meeting ends before we can get there."

"What do you mean 'we'?"

"I just mean the Roman authorities."

"Are you one of the Roman authorities?"

"No, I told you, I'm an architect."

"This is fascinating," Tamara said with some excitement. "Can I see one of these caves?"

Giorgio regarded her closely then replied, "Yes, I suppose so."

Circus Maximus, Rome

September 1985

Giorgio hailed a cab and they got in the seat behind the driver.

"*Circo Massimo*," he said to the driver. "This is one of Rome's most famous tourist spots..." he began.

"Yes, I know," Tamara chimed in. "The Circus Maximus is where the great chariot races took place."

"Ah, *sì*, but tourists don't know that it is famous also for the Mithraeum that is there. This is one of, oh, maybe thirty or forty Mithraea in Rome. But it is very well preserved."

"Are there signs that the terrorists have used it?" She was now intrigued, and a bit fearful, that this extremist group had worked their way into Rome.

"No. This is too important to the people of Rome. This Mithraea is well watched. All activities are supervised here and entrance is not allowed except by the authorities."

"But how can we get in there then?"

"It's not so hard," Giorgio assured her. "I can take care of it."

While they rode over the stones of the ancient city of Rome, Tamara remained in awe of her surroundings. It truly was the Eternal City, and the realization that caves such as these existed below the surface just made the adventure even more exciting.

"Why would the terrorists come here?"

"Well, for one thing, the early Mithraists were from Persia," he began.

"But I thought you said 'maybe.' "

"No, I don't think it's Greece, or Turkey. I think it's Persia. We know of a Hezbollah-affiliated group called CSPPA – it's a long title, but let's just use that, CSPPA – and their pledge has long been to 'destroy Rome.' "

"They said that? I hadn't heard about terrorists targeting Rome before," Tamara said with some concern in her voice. "Why Rome?"

"To say 'Rome' was long thought just to be a symbol of Western Civilization. The CSPPA wanted to attack and defeat the West, and they referred to Rome when they said that.

"At first, when the anti-Western terrorist movement grew large and strong, the Roman authorities thought we might be under imminent attack. But as the group spread its war over the Middle East, many people came to understand that references to Rome were really just symbolic references to the West, so we relaxed."

"But you said they're here."

"Yes, they're here now. So, we now think that CSPPA is planning something, maybe something emblematic, to attack Rome and take their stand here against the West and what they believe it has done to their own civilization."

"But this – what did you call it? CSPPA – is failing, right?" Tamara asked hopefully. "They're being defeated."

"This is true, but sometimes a defeated army becomes desperate and is willing to make grand statements of their power, recessive though it may be, before their final death throes."

About then, the driver pulled to the curb at a stone wall with an opening in it leading to a set of downward facing steps. Giorgio paid the cabbie and they left the car and started toward the steps.

A man stood at the entrance and while he didn't seem to be a government official, he did command the door as if he was responsible for all who entered. Tamara wondered if he could be over-powered by the terrorists whose figures she now held firmly in her imagination, but he simply accepted Giorgio's salutation. The two of them were admitted to the underground space and walked gingerly down the stone steps leading to the interior.

Soft LED lighting illuminated the interior and when Tamara's eyes adjusted, she began to see that there were several rooms below ground. Each room had grottoes cut into the side walls, some featuring artwork that focused on a man battling a bull. He rode the animal's back, and had his left hand in the bull's nostrils, while he drew a knife across the exposed throat of the beast.

"That's Mithras," said Giorgio. "This is an iconic representation. He slays the beast – that's their enemy – and castrates it." At that, Giorgio pointed to the snake at the bull's feet, a serpent biting the testicles of the great animal.

"But who is the Mithraists' enemy?"

Giorgio shrugged his shoulders.

"Maybe, in ancient times, it was the Roman soldiers. Maybe, today, it's the world."

They walked through the space unaccompanied by the door minder, and Tamara enjoyed the audio tour that Giorgio was providing. She noticed that the grottoes were all arranged as raised platforms, with the statue or artwork centered on the dais, and an arch cut into the stone overhead.

"There's your arch," she said, jabbing Giorgio in the ribs.

"Yes, well, that one is carved into the stone, and it is harder to collapse. Not like the arches built up from the ground with many individual stones."

Still, Tamara saw him cast an architect's eye on the curve of the arch.

Via Veneto, Rome

September 1985

They spent Tamara's last evening in Rome walking up and down the Via Veneto. This avenue had long been the popular address for international stores, and the lights from the shops gleamed in multi-colors against the dark, starry night. Tamara held Giorgio's hand, pressing a bit tighter than usual, as if to hold on to him as long, and as firmly, as possible.

They planned her return visit, once again six months hence, but this time their plans were more serious and, yet, more exciting.

"You can come back," Giorgio began, "in six months, yes?"

Tamara nodded and smiled, squeezing his fingers in hers.

"Yes, of course," she added, as a teardrop formed on her lower eyelid. "But I don't want to go now."

Giorgio returned her embrace as they walked further down the street.

He paused briefly at the door to a wine bar, and then pulled Tamara inside. They walked up to the bar rather than take a seat, and ordered glasses of wine. He asked for a San Giusto Chianti Classico and, hearing that, Tamara simply nodded yes, holding up two fingers.

"Why stand?" she asked.

"We can do this like the Romans do," as he waved his hand at the crowd. The bar he chose was very crowded, the tables all taken, and those standing at the bar were three-deep.

"We can have a glass of wine here, rub elbows with this happy crowd, and then move on to another."

"Bar-hopping, huh?" she asked. "Great way to spend my last night in Rome."

They sipped their wine and made attempts at conversation, but the decibel level of the cross conversations was too much. Giorgio took one last draught of his wine, emptying the glass, and crooked a finger at Tamara to indicate that they should leave.

Once outside, she slipped her hand through Giorgio's arm and they sauntered along the sidewalk as a couple in love, with smiles on their faces, and at a leisurely pace that showed that they were not trying to get anywhere in particular.

About a block along, Giorgio stopped, spied an empty table at a quiet sidewalk café, and immediately commandeered Tamara in its direction.

"I thought we were going to do as the Romans do," she inquired.

"Those Romans," he responded, yanking his thumb back in the direction of the bar they had just left, "are too loud, and too young." But he laughed as they settled into the table at the café. "No, they're fine. I just wanted to have a bit more quiet time with you before you leave."

The thought of her flight the next day brought that tear back out on her eyelid, and Tamara reached up quickly to brush it away with her hand.

Giorgio ordered a Negroni. Tamara knew she should avoid strong drinks in her current fragile state of mind, so she ordered a glass of Prosecco, although she did steal a sip of Giorgio's drink.

"Whew, that's good!" she expressed with a smile, but then settled for her sparkling wine.

"When I come back, will you still marry me?"

"Oh, *mi'amore*, of course," said Giorgio, gripping her hand in his.

"Where?"

"Ha, ha! Do you need reassurance?"

"Yes, I do!"

"You don't believe me?"

"Yes, I believe you, but I want to have an image in my head, to keep me happy while I wait for the next one hundred eighty days to pass."

"I thought we could go to my home in Florence, where my family is. I want to have us wed in that city. Is this okay with you?"

Tamara's eyes softened, then filled with tears.

"Yes, that's so okay with me," was all she could get out.

Dinner with Julie

March 2017

Julie was very quiet during my description of that night with Giorgio. Putting me – her mother – in a place with an early lover, and that place being the wondrous city of Rome, and conjuring images of me marrying this man in Florence, under the Tuscan sun, made this tale so much more real for her.

"You went back," she said haltingly.

I just nodded.

Julie had no way of knowing before this evening that there had been a wedding in my life before I met her father. Most kids seem to have trouble grasping images of their parents from the time before their marriage. It's completely normal, and our kids' own lives and loves prove it, but somehow the romantic life of their parents, particularly if it involves a series of romances, are often unmentioned.

She didn't have much to say, and I didn't know how to bring the conversation into the present, so I returned to the past.

Leonardo da Vinci Airport, Rome

March 1986

Tamara had barely gotten through customs when she could see Giorgio on the other side of the barrier waving to her. He smiled when he got her attention, then waited for her to get through the gate and to where he stood.

A long embrace followed while crowds of weary Americans tromped past them in search of luggage on the revolving carriage. After a moment, they separated slightly, shared a kiss, and Giorgio looked longingly into Tamara's eyes.

"The trip, it was okay?" he asked.

"Long, and it seemed longer than usual," she admitted with a grin.

Giorgio loosened his grip on her waist and turned them in the direction of the baggage claim area. Tamara soon picked up the two suitcases she had brought along, and they exited the building. There was a man standing next to Giorgio's Fiat, which was parked at the curb. Giorgio thanked him and shook his hand, and the man disappeared into the throng of travelers. As they slipped into Giorgio's car, Tamara shot a quizzical glance in his direction.

"Who was that?"

"Oh, just a car minder," he replied.

"A what?"

"A car minder. I get someone to stand next to my car, act like it's his, so the police won't tow it away. So I can have my car waiting for me."

Tamara laughed at this very Roman solution.

"But he seemed like he knew you. It wasn't just someone standing there when you pulled up, was it?"

"No, not just a stranger. I know him. It's Tino, a colleague."

"An architect?"

"No, a colleague. It's complicated," he added, but felt the need to change the subject.

"So, we go to Firenze, yes?"

The new topic of conversation changed her mood, and Tamara excitedly nodded yes.

The distance to Florence was not great, but first Giorgio had to navigate the highways at and around the airport, a process that might take as long as the journey itself to Florence. He rounded the long, curving roadway and headed toward A90, the multi-lane highway that rings Rome. As they drove closer to the city itself, Giorgio aimed his car toward A90 north to put them in the direction of central Tuscany.

Along the way, they could see a long aqueduct that pointed toward Rome. Giorgio drove in silence but Tamara gazed out at the ancient structure, a magnificent accomplishment for the early empire to draw water from the mountains and run it all the way down the peninsula to Rome itself. While it wasn't a terribly complicated structure – the aqueduct consisted of a few layers of huge stone troughs standing one above the other – it was massive in length and height. She took special note of the enormous arches that supported the entire structure, and smiled at Giorgio when she thought about the pride he seemed to take in describing this particular architectural component.

They took the A90 around the city and then the SR2 going north into the countryside. The green, rolling hills of Tuscany took over the landscape and Tamara looked fondly at them. Whether she and Giorgio ended up here or in America had not yet been discussed, but the verdant farmland and old stone homes that dotted the landscape of Tuscany bid her welcome, and she was slowly convincing herself – without his prompting – that this is where they should settle.

Tamara had been to Florence before, long before she met Giorgio, and they had not come there together yet. This was her first trip to his ancestral land, and the thought of it made her nerves tingle. Giorgio continued driving in silence, but Tamara's mind was buzzing with thoughts of their marriage and life together.

At Home in Florence

March 1986

After a while, Giorgio pulled off the main highway and merged onto a narrow, two-lane road heading toward the east, skirting Florence on the south, and around toward the city from that angle. Tamara had succumbed to jet lag and, with the light breeze coming through the window, had slept for the last thirty minutes. Giorgio looked over at her and smiled, but didn't want to disturb her. The act of turning off the highway jostled her just a bit, though, to wake her. She straightened up in the seat, adjusted the belt so it wasn't pulled too tight against her chest, and threw a sleepy look at Giorgio.

"Sorry," she said, "I guess I dozed off."

"It's okay. I'm glad you slept. We're almost there."

Giorgio took the roads into Florence masterfully. From long practice, he knew which streets would move fast and which would require him to double back. He also knew how to handle the wheel to produce the most efficient passage through intersections that were bottled up with pedestrians. Once or twice, he swerved gently around street vendors hawking their wares on the sidewalk, and more than twice to avoid striking a tourist who stepped off the curb without looking.

He rounded a corner and pulled the Fiat to a stop at a curb. A curved "24" was displayed on a terra cotta sign next to an intricately carved wooden door, and Giorgio popped out of the driver's seat and quickly moved toward the trunk of his car. Tamara emerged from the vehicle a bit more slowly, still waking from her rest and recovering from her flight. By the time she was on the curb,

Giorgio had put the two suitcases down next to her, as they both heard the door of the home swing open.

"*Ah, Giorgio, è quasi ora!*" the woman exclaimed – "It's about time!" But despite upbraiding her son, Etta went straight for Tamara, wrapping her in an embrace and talking so quickly that it made Tamara dizzy.

"Tamara, this is mama," Giorgio added, as if there was any doubt. Etta had a full head of hair, grey but boundlessly curly, and an array of wrinkles at the corners of her mouth and eyes that displayed for everyone that her smile was permanently fixed on her face.

"*Mama, sì,*" Etta said, pointing to herself, and making no attempt to come up with another moniker for Tamara to use.

"*Ciao... mama...*" but Tamara had to pause before uttering the second word. Nevertheless, Etta beamed at being called by the familiar term, then turned quickly back toward the door, taking Tamara by the arm and ushering her inside. Giorgio was left on the sidewalk to deal with the suitcases.

Etta continued a steady stream of words, requiring Giorgio to catch up and help with translation.

"Mama doesn't speak English too well..." he began before his mother interrupted.

"I speak okay English," she corrected her son, then turned to Tamara. "It's okay, yes?"

"Yes, I mean, *sì.* No wait, I mean yes," Tamara fumbled, and Etta beamed again.

"*Ma preferisco l'italiano,*" she said with a wave of the hand - "But I prefer Italian" – wherewith she launched back into another stream. She was describing her house to Tamara, interspersing the description with explanations of food which her guest took to mean what they were going to eat that day. Then Etta turned back toward furniture, the "*glorioso*" photograph of her late husband on the wall over the hutch, all the while leading Tamara toward the steps near the back of the room.

Plunging ahead up the steps and pulling Tamara along with her, Etta never stopped talking. Occasionally Tamara looked over her shoulder at Giorgio who just smiled and shrugged his shoulders as if to say, "This is the way it is."

At the top of the stairway, Etta pointed left and pulled Tamara into a brightly lit room with white-washed walls and colorful pictures of Italy's great edifices hanging there. A small bed sat in the corner, and next to it was a desk with writing materials and a framed photo showing a young Giorgio in school uniform.

"*Quest'è la camera di Giorgio*," she said, "This is Giorgio's room," but acted apologetic. Tamara looked at Giorgio for explanation, and he responded.

"Yes, my room, but only you will be staying here."

"Well, I think I expected that," Tamara said with a slight grin that turned Etta's cheeks pink. "But what about you?"

"I'll sleep downstairs."

"Isn't there another room up here?"

"Yes, but that is mother's. Besides, she wouldn't let us sleep on the same floor." Giorgio threw an obedient, but impish look in his mother's direction. "Not on the same floor," he repeated, and they both tried to hide their smiles.

The next few days went along like that, with Etta jabbering away about Giorgio, their home, and their life in Florence, and Tamara keeping up for a while then falling hopelessly behind. Usually, Giorgio would step in and translate and rescue her, but sometimes he would just let the linguistic snowstorm overwhelm her...and laugh.

His mother was a woman full of energy, and it seemed like it increased throughout the day rather than declining like it does with other people. She talked about her husband, Giorgio's father – Vincenzo – and how he had fought in the "great war" which Giorgio had to translate for Tamara.

"She thinks of World War II as the 'great war' but I know many Americans use that phrase to refer to the first World War in the 19-teens."

Etta also went into particular detail about her son's eating preferences. She wasn't trying to prove that he was a picky eater; rather, she was imparting to Tamara what she needed to know to cook for him.

"Pasta, pasta, pasta," then pausing for the right English to use, "he only wants pasta," wagging her index finger in the air. It was then that Tamara realized where Giorgio got that particular gesture to emphasize a point.

"But he also needs... *che'è la parola, Giorgio*?" – what is the word?

"*Come lo so*?" he asked with a grin – "How do I know?" – "*Che cosa intendi*?"

"*Bistecca, vitello, pollo...*"

"*Ah, sì*," and then turning to Tamara he said, "She says I also want meat."

"Yeah," she responded, "I've seen. How do I say, 'no shit' in Italian?"

But she didn't have too. Etta heard her words and covered her mouth to hide her giggling.

Wandering the Streets of Florence

March 1986

Fortunately, there were times they left the house and toured Firenze, leaving the translation difficulties behind. Giorgio took her to the Ponte Vecchio where a teeming throng of tourists crowded the stone mantle of the bridge for photos. There the jewelry shops abounded, with exquisite gold and rare stones, but all for a rich man's purse.

"If you want jewelry, I'll buy it, but not here," said Giorgio. "It's a beautiful place, but the prices are *piu caro*" – "very dear."

They went to the Piazza della Repubblica for the midday meal. Here, back at home, Giorgio had trouble using American words like "lunch," even for Tamara's benefit. He felt like he was back in his element, and the word was *pranzo* or midday meal, not "lunch." They sat at Caffé Gilli, a still-famous restaurant that dominated the square.

"The food here is good, but not the American menu," Giorgio said, pointing to the specialties that he most preferred. They ordered house wine, something that shocked Tamara but Giorgio explained that, here, in his home, all the wine was good. Tamara could see that his pride rose to stratospheric heights the closer he drew to the magnet called Firenze.

The food of Florence was different than that of Rome. Of course, anything *alla fiorentina* was expected to be superb, and Giorgio ordered *bistecca alla fiorentina* – beefsteak florentine – to prove the point. Tamara had filled up on mama's food for the last few days, so she began this next meal with *briciolata*, a broth soup with crumbled ricotta and small slices of toasted bread. She had to promise Giorgio that she would order more – and not go hungry – so she also asked for *pappardelle sulla lepre*, a bowl of broad noodles dressed with a rabbit sauce.

The wine was just what Tamara expected, simple and satisfying, exactly as Giorgio had described it. The hot broth soup was soothing, and the pasta filled her up. Meanwhile, she watched Giorgio devour a large beefsteak served with a side of broccolini and sautéed, sliced garlic.

"Is this the way you eat when you're at home?" she asked.

"All food is good in Tuscany," he bragged. "Well, also in Italy, but this..." he said pointing to the slab of meat on his plate – "is the best."

"Where do we go from here?"

Tamara's question sounded both narrow, and broad, and Giorgio was momentarily stumped, trying to decide whether she meant what they would do that afternoon, or what they would do with their lives. So he concocted a similar double entendre for her.

"We'll have to just see where life takes us."

Tamara hadn't realized the double meaning of her question, but laughed with him. Then, she pursued the unasked question.

"When?" The rest of the question was obvious, and Giorgio knew that she didn't mean touring.

"I was thinking of a ceremony on the top of the hill over there, vaguely waving in the direction of the Arno River. He had pointed out the Piazzale di Michelangelo to her earlier while they stood on the Ponte Vecchio. The piazza above the hill on the other side of the river held a commanding view of the city of Florence, and he said that sunsets there are spectacular.

"When?" she repeated.

He paused only for a moment.

"I thought we should do it this Saturday, in three days."

A tingle went down Tamara's spine as she realized that this idea of hers was coming true. Then she leaned over her edge of the table to plant a kiss on Giorgio's mouth.

"*D'accordo*," she said with a smile – "agreed."

He laid his fork down on the plate and took a gulp of wine before continuing, and Tamara recognized a hesitation in his action.

"I have to return to Rome tonight."

"Why?" Tamara couldn't keep the sound of alarm out of her voice.

"It's just business. Would you come with me?"

That relieved her concern, and of course she wouldn't want to stay with mama while Giorgio was back in Rome.

"What's happening?"

"Nothing, really. Just work." He was never very forthcoming about his work, other than telling Tamara that he was an architect. She had once pressed him for a tour of the buildings he had worked on, but he laughed and just said, "All my work is in the details, in the structure, in the interior. You couldn't see it from the street."

At his home in Florence, she had seen his drawings and school memorabilia, and Etta had gone on rapturously about Giorgio's accomplishments as an architect. And he even kept a framed copy of his university certificate in that room in Florence.

He was certainly an architect. She was sure of it. Or so Tamara had told herself.

"Well, at least he's not married," she thought one day while listening to Etta's litany of her son's life.

The next morning, they packed their bags and piled into Giorgio's little Fiat. Etta stood on the doorstep with a mother's tears in her eyes, waving as the little car rolled across the cobblestoned street and out of sight.

Dinner with Julie

March 2017

"What was it, mom?"

Telling the story of Giorgio's mother, his home, and our return to Rome had put me in a state of memory that shut out the present. I knew my voice was still working, but I was so immersed in the meaning of what I was saying that I forgot my audience was my daughter.

"We went back to Rome, it was just a couple of hours away and I thought we'd be there for a night or two. We already planned the wedding and would need to be back by Saturday anyway. Actually, I enjoyed the thought that I could have Giorgio to myself again, and be able to sleep with him again.

"So, we arrived in Rome and went straight to his apartment. I had been there before and gave him a hard time about how stark it was.

"'Why don't you have more furniture,' I told him, 'and some pictures on the walls?' "

"I kidded him that he needed a woman's touch, some decorating to make life more colorful, and bearable. He laughed back at me and reminded me that he was a bachelor, and besides we would be living in Florence."

"'What's the point of decorating this room now,' he said. 'We won't be here long.' "

"I smiled at that, but I suddenly realized that he was packing up his life in Rome. I wanted to ask if it was to move to the States or back to Florence, but a knock came at the door.

"When he opened it, I saw Tino, the man who was Giorgio's car minder at the airport. I thought he was just a passing acquaintance of Giorgio's but now I realized that they worked together.

"'I have to go,'" he told me, kissing me on the cheek and whisking out the doorway. He paused just a second before closing it, throwing a brilliant smile back in my direction."

"What was it, mom?" Julie repeated.

"Work, honey. Just like Giorgio said."

Dinner with Julie

March 2017

"But he didn't come home for dinner that night," I told my daughter.

"I started to worry when night fell and I hadn't heard from him.

"We didn't have cell phones back then, so I thought I should stay in his apartment. At least it had a phone and Giorgio would try to reach me there. I couldn't leave the apartment.

"I stayed there all night, alone, and never heard from him. The sounds of the street were the same, although now they seemed louder to me. I was searching for any sign, any clue that he was nearby, and my sense of hearing became so acute that I could hear the creaking of the boards from the apartment next to ours. Once I thought I heard the sound come from the hallway so I rushed to the door and flung it open.

"There was no one there. I had expected someone – had hoped for Giorgio – but there was no one."

Julie remained silent. She knew that any question she wanted to ask would be answered by me anyway without prompting.

"I fell asleep in the chair with a thin blanket pulled over me. Once, when it slipped to the floor, the chill in the room woke me and I sat straight up, realizing that I had been dozing, and wondering what I might have missed.

"I ran to the bedroom but he wasn't there. Of course not. If Giorgio had returned he would not have left me to sleep in the chair. So I went to the door and pulled it open. In the dead of night, with the hallway sconces turned low, the light in the corridor gave me a frightful feeling, so I closed the door and huddled close once again in the chair."

Julie gulped and, in the silence that had settled over us, I could hear the swallow go down her throat.

"I fell asleep again, but it was a fitful sleep. I tossed and turned, waking myself too often, then crashing again in a mixture of exhaustion and fear.

"My eyes were open and staring at the window when the first rays of blue light crept up the panes of glass. I don't know if I even blinked; my eyes were so dry they ached. I pulled myself up from the chair and paced back and forth around the apartment. I checked the bedroom and bathroom again, thinking that somehow Giorgio would appear in a place I hadn't checked. But I had…and he wasn't there.

"I rummaged around his apartment for information about his firm, an invoice, a paystub, anything that would have an office phone number to call. I was astonished at how little paper he had there. There were no bills, not paystubs…nothing. Then I found a slip of paper in a drawer of his desk. It had Tino's name written on it, a phone number, and then another phone number below it.

"First, I called the number next to Tino's name. It rang four times and a greeting in Italian told me that 'no one was home…please leave a message.' "

"So I called the second number. After the second ring a young woman's voice answered."

" '*L'Ufficio del Architetto Ramboli*,' she said.

"May I speak with Giorgio?" I asked.

"*No, mi dispiace* – I'm sorry – he is not in. Giorgio is on a leave of absence from the firm."

"Leave of absence? What for?" I asked incredulously.

Suddenly the voice on the line brightened.

"He's getting married!"

"I know he's getting married. I'm his fiancé," I replied.

The voice got even more excited.

"*La fidanzata*!" she exclaimed with joy. "You must be so happy, congratu…."

I hung up the phone halfway through her excited response. I didn't need to hear any more of that. I needed to know where Giorgio was.

So I was left to wait, again. And I had to stay in the apartment. If Giorgio was in trouble – and there must have been trouble or he wouldn't leave me like this – I needed to be where Giorgio could reach me.

The Apartment, Rome

March 1986

Tamara was slowly becoming terrified that something awful had happened to Giorgio. She paced around the apartment all day, so much that she forgot to eat and couldn't even sit for more than a few minutes at a time.

She was alone at precisely the time in her life that she had become convinced that she would never be alone again.

Giorgio didn't call that day, and by nightfall she regretted hanging up on the woman at his office. Maybe she could have gotten more information from her. Tamara picked up the phone to see if she could trace Etta... surely, she would have a telephone. But she lowered the receiver to the stand, wondering what she would say to a woman whose only son had suddenly gone missing. And, worse, figure out how to say it in Italian.

It occurred to her that she had never met anyone in Giorgio's life except his mother. No friends, no colleagues – well, there was Tino, but she could hardly say she had met him. Tamara was so happy in Giorgio's presence that she never realized that they were a world of two people. That night she realized that this was too small a world and, when the connection is broken, she was adrift and lonely.

Tamara had never felt this lonely.

She passed another night as before, sleeping poorly in a chair with a thin blanket offering little comfort. She resolved to awake the next morning and be more aggressive in her search. She couldn't continue to sit and wait. If she had to, Tamara would leave the apartment and go in search of Giorgio.

But first, she had to get through the night.

Dinner with Julie

March 2017

I looked over at Julie and her eyes were red. Her lower lip quivered ever so slightly and she moved her chair closer to mine to comfort me.

"I didn't see him that night, Julie, or the next day.

"My spirits sank as I faced the prospect that Giorgio was gone, or lost, or taken."

I had known him for a year, although we only spent about four weeks of it together. But I knew him. I could tell from his touch, his smile, and the soft sparkle in his eyes that he cared deeply for me. But now he was gone.

Where? That was the question.

The Apartment, Rome

March 1986

Tamara spent the next day walking around Rome. She had a picture of Giorgio, one of those wacky, over-smiling photos you surrender to when you're swept off your feet, so she showed it to people.

They were all strangers to her – she didn't know anyone in the city – and most shook their heads '*no*' when she asked about him. She pulled the phone number from her pocket and searched her memory for the woman's voice when she called.

"*L'Ufficio del Architetto Ramboli*," she had said.

Tamara borrowed a phone book from a little coffee shop and found the address for Giorgio's firm. It was not far so she walked – well, ran – to the appointed street.

The same lilting voice from the phone greeted her at the reception desk, but the lady was a bit less friendly. When she introduced herself – *la fidanzata di Giorgio* – the receptionist frowned, probably remembering how Tamara had hung the phone up on her.

"Let me explain," she pleaded. "I can't find Giorgio. You know him, I know him. He's a gentle man. An honest man. I haven't seen him in two days. There must be something wrong."

She looked up at Tamara with little compassion. She could tell she was wondering whether Giorgio had fled this strange American woman.

"He is on a leave of absence," was all she would tell Tamara, who quickly concluded that this would be the barrier to further communication. He had taken the leave of absence to marry her, but now the woman before her wondered if her friend's leave had a fuller, more personal agenda. And she wasn't going to give anything away.

"What if I told you Giorgio was in trouble," Tamara said. If she cared about him, she might be swayed by that.

"You know him. I know him. Giorgio doesn't just disappear."

The woman thought about this for a while, but concluded that she was unable – or unwilling – to contribute anything more.

"Was anyone here invited to his wedding?" Tamara asked. She thought a co-worker or friend might have some information.

"Yes, Raffaele," the receptionist offered, "but he said the wedding would be in Firenze," and looking at the calendar on her desk, added, "tomorrow. So Raffaele is already gone too."

"Do you know Tino?" Tamara asked.

She gave a quizzical look.

"No. Who is he?"

"I don't really know. Okay, this Raffaele. How can I find him?"

"I suppose he has gone to Firenze, to Giorgio's house," but she stopped short then. The look in her face suggested that she was suddenly nervous that she was giving up too much.

After that, Tamara gave up on his office, but planned to find Raffaele – and confront Etta if she had to.

Florence

March 1986

She rented a car and drove the two hours to Florence. It might have been longer, but her white-knuckle speeds got her there faster than Giorgio had, even with his driving. In a brief lightness of being, she smiled thinking that Giorgio would be proud of the way she whirled through the lanes of traffic, but then her mood turned dark again.

In Florence, Tamara had the task of hunting down Giorgio's house. She hadn't paid much attention when they arrived the last time; she was jet-lagged. The sweet fresh air had put her to sleep and she didn't watch for the turns and intersections. But she had spent a few days wandering the streets of the city with Giorgio and had learned how to walk back to Etta's house.

Realizing that the path from the Piazza della Signoria was one they traveled several times, Tamara drove as close as she could to that square, then retraced their steps while driving the rental car.

Two streets up, a left turn, and five streets – or, wait, was it six? – then another few blocks that led closer to the Arno River, then a sudden turn down a narrow via. Tamara looked up at the walls of the homes on either side and smiled for the first time in days. Etta's light blue cooking smock hung from the rope outside her upstairs window. Tamara had seen her don the smock each morning, cook all day, then wash and hang the smock out of the window every evening. This was definitely Etta's house.

But it was mid-afternoon. Etta always had her smock on throughout the day. She would be cooking or cleaning. The sky-blue smock would not still be hanging in the street, so Tamara hurried toward the door with the curved "24" displayed on a terra cotta sign.

She paused on the stoop, gathered herself and rehearsed her lines once more before knocking. Lifting her right hand and closing it in a fist, she rapped lightly on the carved wooden door. There was no sound at first, then feet padding in her direction. They sounded heavy, heavier than Etta's.

Were they Giorgio's?

The door swung open and there stood Tino, two steps above Tamara and towering over her. He did not smile, but his face showed no malice. This was their first close-up meeting but Tamara soon concluded that Tino was not an angry man...just very serious.

"Is Giorgio here?"

Tino shook his head, no.

"May I see Etta?"

Tino didn't respond right away, but looked over his shoulder into the darkened room. With a sigh, and a nod to someone behind him, he opened the door wider and let Tamara in.

Etta sat on the couch in the room and rose to greet Tamara.

"Are you alright?" Tamara asked her.

Tamara expected to find Giorgio's mother distraught. With Tino in the room, surely he had already delivered news of Giorgio's disappearance. But Etta was calm, almost cheerful, and Tamara stood in the middle of the room with a confused look on her face.

"Where is Giorgio?" she asked, directing the question at Etta, but panning toward Tino at the same time.

"He has been called away to work," Tino said.

"*Sì*," was all Etta offered, but it seemed like a forced agreement.

"Where is he?" Tamara repeated. "I have a right to know."

Then Tino and Etta came to her and held her close.

"Yes, you do," Tino said in an oblique offering. "But not now."

"Why not now? We're getting married tomorrow!"

Tino and Etta looked at each other, and Etta's eyes filled with tears.

"He will find you," she said to Tamara.

"Yes, he will find you," repeated Tino.

Dinner with Julie

March 2017

"Mom, this is horrible! What happened? You saw him again, right?"

"Yes, I did," I told her, comforting Julie with a smile and a pat on her hand.

Leonardo da Vinci Airport, Rome

March 1986

By Tino's telling, Giorgio had been called away to work. Etta just nodded her head as Tino continued with his story, occasionally looking at him as if some specific detail was news to her also.

Tamara listened carefully, but felt that the story Tino was telling was short on specifics and long on reassurances.

"Giorgio is an important person, he has important things to do," Tino said.

"He said he was an architect," Tamara protested.

"And he is," declared Tino.

"But why does an architect disappear?"

"Oh, he didn't disappear. We know where he is."

"That's not fair," Tamara raged, jumping to her feet. "Why won't you tell me where he is?"

"That wouldn't be a good thing right now. But he will find you," Tino repeated.

Tamara sat down again and sunk deeper into the chair. Etta reached over and held her hand, and Tamara looked up at the old woman's face. The wrinkled brow, the soft gray eyes, the unkempt hair – Tamara took it all in, but still tried to understand why Etta wasn't terrified at what she knew, or what she didn't know about her son.

Tamara sat quietly for a long time, Etta looked down at her hands, and Tino studied the two women in silence. Nothing was said for about thirty minutes, until Tamara stood up and peered directly at Tino.

"Will you tell me anything more? Now?"

He returned her stare, shaking his head.

"Then what am I supposed to do?" she asked.

Tino looked directly at her, considered her question, but could only offer a blank and wordless response.

Tears of frustration brimmed at her eyelids, and Tamara spun on her heel and walked out the door. She got into the rental car and pulled away from the curb. After about three blocks, the emotion had welled up in her to the breaking point. Tamara yanked the car to a stop and buried her head in her hands, sobbing so hard that her chest hurt.

She waited another two days in Giorgio's apartment, with nowhere to go and no idea what to do next. When she didn't hear from him, Tamara began to consider going back to the States. She didn't want to give up, but she was no longer really searching for him; she was just clinging to the fading hope that Giorgio would walk through the door and everything would go back to what she remembered...and had planned.

On Wednesday, March 26, she packed her bags, leaned them up against the couch, and turned to stare at the gloomy, quiet apartment around her. She had searched every nook and cranny of the three rooms there, even peering into the various sections of the refrigerator and freezer in the hope that Giorgio had hid clues there. She had his paystub that she found earlier, and she had placed another fruitless call to his office.

"I told you already, he's on a leave of absence to be married!" was the terse reply.

Anger rose in Tamara's throat when she heard that. She wanted to scream back that she was Giorgio's fiancé and that he damn well wasn't on leave to get married.

But on this day, she had tried everything, and found nothing. Tino's words returned to her – "He will find you" – but now the phrase offered little solace.

With one more look around the apartment, Tamara pulled on the doorknob and dragged her suitcase out into the hallway. Down past the two other apartments on that floor, down the one flight of steps to the street, and into the taxi she hailed.

"*Aeroporto, per favore*," she said glumly.

It all seemed like such a defeat. She felt scared, emotionally drained, and abandoned. She was alternately angry at and worried about Giorgio. She didn't know whether to fight or cry, but her tears had dried up and she sat looking out the window of the cab, more unsure of her future than on any other day in her life.

The airport wasn't near but in her distracted state the minutes evaporated quickly, so she hardly noticed when the car pulled up to the sidewalk outside the Alitalia airlines desk. The driver retrieved her luggage from the trunk, took her money, and waved goodbye.

All of this seemed so normal that it reminded Tamara of how abnormal it all really was. She had come to Italy to marry Giorgio and, now, she didn't even know where he was.

Her semi-conscious state of mind continued through check-in and lining up to board the flight home. If anyone paid attention, they might have thought she was mentally damaged, so distant and unaware she was of her surroundings. But no one paid any attention. Tamara was the only one occupying the world she was now in.

She stood in the short line of people flying to Dulles Airport near Washington, D.C., people who were going home or people who were embarking on a vacation. The television was tuned to a local news station and behind the news desk were two men reporting on the events of the day.

Tamara's Italian had improved but she wasn't fluent. The raised voices of the newsmen got her attention, though, and dragged her reluctantly into the present.

"*La bomba è esplosa sotto terra,*" one newscaster said. "The bomb exploded underground."

People in the line moved toward the jetway to the plane, but Tamara stood still.

"*Era nel mitraeo.*" – "It was in the mithraeum."

The television screen switched to a police officer standing before a bank of microphones. He was addressing a large crowd gathered on the steps of some unidentified white marble building.

"*Sappiamo ora La Commissione di Solidarietà con i Prigionieri Politici Arabi e Mediorientali, si chiama CSPPA in Inglese.*"

Tamara had to repeat the phrase twice in her head to translate it. "The Commission of Solidarity with Arab and Middle East Political Prisoners, known as CSPPA in English."

By now the line had nearly passed her and was boarding the plane, and Tamara was called to the desk by the agent with her hand out, waiting to be given Tamara's boarding pass.

There was a bombing at a mithraeum, and apparently it killed a number of terrorists associated with this CSPPA.

One agent took Tamara by the elbow, and the other one took the pass that Tamara held lightly between her thumb and forefinger. Her attention was still on the television screen, even though she was being ushered forward and out of a straight line of sight to the broadcast.

A picture of the mithraeum appeared on the screen, obviously one taken before the blast, then it switched to a contemporaneous photograph of the mouth of the ancient cave. The arched stone opening of the original was replaced by a solid wall of stone and earth that had collapsed and closed off the portal of the mithraeum, entombing the ancient relics inside.

"*Molti terroristi sono stati riuniti li, e tutti sono morti in esplosione*," he reported. "Many terrorists were gathered there, and they all died in the explosion."

As Tamara was being pulled toward the plane, she reached for one more glance at the television screen. She saw the arch of the mithraeum. Giorgio's words spoken at the *Campidoglio* came back to her.

"Arches are the most vulnerable place in a building. Designed properly, and protected, the opening is safe. Mistakes in the design, even subtle mistakes not caught by the architect in time, and the building can come down in a heap."

But there was an explosion, Tamara thought, as she was pushed toward the portal of the airplane.

Dinner with Julie

March 2017

"I boarded the plane that day," I told my daughter. "But I was in a state of shock and confusion. I couldn't stop thinking about the arch that was the opening to that mithraeum, and Giorgio's warning about its strength. But I also recalled his words about terrorists, and how they sometimes gathered in these vacated spaces, the ancient mithraea of Rome, to plot acts of violence against society.

Julie looked at me with a look of helplessness. Not knowing what to say, she let me continue.

"When I got home I began researching this CSPPA. They arose suddenly in 1985 and spread their influence, gaining recruits quickly. As I paged through the news clippings, I found a variety of attacks they had conducted in Europe, mostly in Paris.

"They attacked a high-speed train in France, the Paris-Lyon link, on March 17, about a week before I came home. No one died, but many people were hurt and there was a lot of damage to the train and the rail system.

"A few days later, March 20, they attacked a shopping gallery on the Champs-Élysées. This time the explosion killed two people, and dozens more were injured. That was just four days before I boarded the Alitalia plane to come home.

"The mithraeum was blown up on March 22, the last day I saw Giorgio."

I looked at Julie, staring directly at her, and continued.

"The arch of the mithraeum was brought down in the explosion, burying everyone who might have been inside. The police captain on the television stated that many terrorists were in that cave, and that they perished with the explosion, or were entombed by it."

"What about Giorgio?" asked Julie. "He wasn't hurt. You said you saw him again."

I smiled back at her. Julie's face was radiant with hope. I wanted to tell her more about Giorgio, to complete the circle for her. But also for me.

Dinner with Julie

March 2017

"Your father proposed to me on a bench outside the courthouse in Annapolis. It was a beautiful, sunny afternoon and we had been walking around the town, the marina, and the quaint old streets of the Colonial section of the city. And then we reached this building, a tall, elegant old brick building, so we sat down to rest our feet.

"He surprised me. I was so surprised I said 'yes' immediately."

Julie beamed at the story. She'd heard it before, but in the midst of my long account of Giorgio, I could see that she took comfort in hearing about her father again.

"So, then he says, 'Well, we're right here,' and waved his hand up at the courthouse. I didn't know what he meant at first, then it struck me. Your father wanted to get married right then, right there!" I had to laugh at the memory.

"Did you?"

"Well, Julie, you've seen pictures of our wedding. You know we were married in an old country inn."

"But some people get married twice. Once on the spur of the moment, then again…more formally for the family, right?"

Julie's eyes sparkled at the possibility of her mom and dad diving into a marriage that would grow and prosper for so many years.

"Yeah, well," I began with a pause. "Yeah, we got married right then and there."

"Oh, my God! I knew it!"

And we both shared a laugh.

"And the other ceremony?" she asked.

"That was about three months later, after we had time to organize it, invite people, and talk my mother down from the ceiling."

"Grandma? She was mad?"

"Oh, she liked the idea of me marrying Ted, just not the part of marrying him on the spur of the moment. She had everything planned and insisted on being part of it."

"I'm sure she would have looked forward to helping," Julie added.

"Yeah, about as much as I looked forward to avoiding her help!"

We sat and enjoyed the memories, each wrapped up in different chapters of Ted's life with us.

But, before Ted – and after Ted – there was Giorgio. So, I returned to him to complete the story for Julie.

"I didn't go back to Rome for a long time. Well, other than twice with your dad, once as a couple before you were born, and once with you."

"When I was sixteen," Julie interjected.

"Yes, when you were sixteen."

"But Giorgio wasn't on my mind, especially when I was with you and your dad. After your father died, I spent a lot of lonely nights, for months on end. We did everything together, and by then you had college, and had moved away and I felt like I had lost my best friend. I took a couple of weekend trips with old girlfriends, to Williamsburg and Philadelphia, but the nights seemed long.

"Slowly, I was able to adjust to my new life. Ted – I mean your dad – was a great influence in our lives and we were very lucky to have had him with us for so many years.

"My friend, Silvia – you remember her, right?"

Julie nodded yes.

"She was going to Madrid and wanted company, so I said I'd go along. Your dad and I had traveled overseas occasionally, oh, maybe four or five times, but mostly we stuck to the States. I had never been to Madrid and thought it would be fun."

"Absolutely, I've been there," Julie added. "You would love it."

"Well, I didn't get to go. Silvia's son was away at college and not having a good time of it. About three weeks before we were to leave, he flunked out and was sent home. Silvia figured she better stay home and deal with this, so I had a ticket to Madrid but no one to go with me.

"I didn't know how to speak Spanish, and although Madrid sounded great, I never shook my love of the Italian people. United Airlines said I could switch the ticket to a round-trip to Rome, and I knew I'd feel more at home there, so I did."

Piazza della Repubblica, Rome

September 2016

Tamara sat at a café snuggled in between two buildings on a sunny day in fall. After finishing the midday meal and a glass of wine, she walked into the sunlight and toward the fountain in the middle of the Piazza della Repubblica.

"Tamara."

She heard only the single word but she knew it was Giorgio. A violent chill went down her spine and she turned to see him standing there. The closely cropped beard was a little grayer than she remembered, and his hair was streaked with silver strands.

Tamara stood slowly, and was so emotional that she had to fight back the urge to convulse in tears. She had not returned to Rome to find Giorgio, had not really even thought about him, but there he stood, thirty years after they last spoke to each other.

"What have you done?" she asked, but the words seemed too angry for what she meant, so she began again.

"Where have you been?" Even that didn't seem right. It sounded like something you asked a person who failed to come home last night, but in the moment, Giorgio's sudden reappearance swept away the years and Tamara seemed to be back in 1986, waiting hopefully for his return.

"Tamara," he said again, and then halted. "I am so thankful to see you again."

She wanted to hit him, to swing her arm in a great arc and slap him full across the face. Then to beat her fists into his chest until the ache in her heart was transferred to his.

But she didn't.

They stood a few feet apart, Tamara unwilling to approach Giorgio, and he feeling undeserving of approaching her. She sat back down but didn't take her eyes off of him.

Giorgio moved slowly toward her, respectfully sitting down on the edge of the fountain next to Tamara, and looked into her eyes.

In that quiet moment, she could take in the reality of Giorgio, the man she had fallen in love with, had promised to marry, and had lost in a depressing chain of years that changed her life forever. But in that moment, without yet speaking, she could glean from the soft look in his eyes and his pained smile that he could be forgiven. She needed to know what had happened, but almost in an instant, she had forgiven him.

"I need to know what happened to you," she began, and Giorgio's story began.

Dinner with Giorgio, Rome

September 2016

"What if I told you I was in prison?" he asked. He had been imprisoned, just not in one kept by the authorities.

They were sitting in a restaurant and it seemed so real, so ordinary to Tamara that she had to keep reminding herself she hadn't seen this man in many years.

"It was a long time, and I was fighting for my life and my sanity."

"What were you in prison for?"

After a long pause, Giorgio continued.

"That's where it gets complicated. You know that the Italian government seems to change often," he said, then offered one of his soft chuckles. "Italians like to say that if you don't like the government, wait a few months and it will change."

"What does that have to do with prison?"

Giorgio resettled himself in his chair, took a sip of wine, and began again.

"I was taken into custody for involvement in matters that were, well, let's say illegal."

"When you abandoned me…" Tamara began, but quickly regretted her phrasing. "When you didn't show up, there was a terrorist attack."

"No, not an attack," he corrected. "There might have been an attack, but there wasn't one."

"Were you part of it?"

"No, no. I was not one of the terrorists." It bothered Giorgio a bit that Tamara could have painted him as one of them.

"I was working for another side, but not the government's. The police at the time were doing too little. We had seen terror attacks in Paris at that time..."

"Yes, I know," Tamara interjected. "There were two, right before then."

"Exactly. The government knew about these, but they ignored the possibility that the same group might attack us."

"The CSPPA," Tamara noted. And the sudden recollection startled even her. She hadn't thought about this group for decades, but the initials tumbled right out of her mouth as if this dinner were being held that very night that Giorgio had disappeared.

"Yes, that was their name. But, so, terror groups change like the Italian government does. There's no more CSPPA, but there are others. Anyway, back to what I was saying. When I tried to stop these terrorists, well...let me begin again. We were..."

"Who's we?"

"Me, and others," Giorgio replied, instinctively reluctant to give up any more names.

"We were part of an opposition group. We were following the CSPPA's actions and warning the government, but we were getting nowhere with them. So, we decided to take matters into our own hands."

He sipped a little more wine, and Tamara stared expectantly at him.

"We found where they were hiding and...we took action...to remove the threat."

"There was a bomb," Tamara added. "An explosion."

"Yes, there was. But I had nothing to do with that."

"But the bomb was put in the arched opening of the mithraeum," she said.

Looking down at his hands, Giorgio nodded.

"You're an architect, and if I remember correctly, you were especially interested in arches. In the strength – or weakness – of them."

"It was only a small bomb, too small to hurt anyone."

"Directly," Tamara said.

"What?"

"I said it was too small to hurt anyone directly."

Giorgio nodded, as if relieved to have that said openly.

"But with the right information," she continued, "that small bomb could be put in exactly the perfect spot to bring the arch down on the portal to the mithraeum, blocking the entrance, and burying everyone inside alive.

"Where were you in prison? What's that about?"

"It was more like hiding, but it was like…what do you Americans call it? Witness protection? The opposition group that I had helped – I promise you, Tamara, they didn't tell me what the bomb would do – they took me away so I'd be safe from the government and the terrorists."

"Why the government?" she asked.

"Well, blowing things up in their city is frowned upon here, don't you think? Especially if it's an ancient artifact like a mithraeum. After a few years it seemed to be safe, so I worked my way back into society."

"With the same name? Wouldn't that be dangerous?"

"Oh, *certo*." Again, that soft chuckle. "No, I have a new name. It's Dante."

"Like in the rings of hell," she responded in sarcasm.

Dinner with Giorgio, Rome

September 2016

"What if I told you I was married?"

Tamara let out a long sigh.

"Well, to tell you the truth…" she began.

"Yes, I know. You were, or you should have been married."

"No, wait, I wasn't married when I met you," she corrected.

"Oh, of course not, neither was I," Giorgio said quickly. "That's not what I meant. I mean when I was freed – and it had been a long time – I didn't think I could call you. I didn't know what I would say. As the years went by, I married, and then I certainly couldn't call you."

"Who is she?"

"Was. Celia and I were married for seven years, but she died in an automobile crash, outside of Perugia."

For the first time since they had met that afternoon, Tamara reached out to touch Giorgio, or Dante.

"I'm sorry," she said, laying her fingers lightly on his forearm.

Giorgio's shrug was one-shouldered, as if the typical Italian gesture for "whatever" required too much effort in the midst of his grief.

"And you? You said you were married," he continued.

Tamara straightened and began. She felt an immediate need to tell Giorgio how happy her marriage had been, and how wonderful her daughter was. She didn't want him to think she had pined for him over the years. In truth, she had successfully forgotten Giorgio once her life took on a new meaning with Ted and Julia.

She told him all of this – all except for the part about forgetting him – and emphasized the happiness she felt in her life and her daughter's success.

"And your husband?" he asked.

"Ted. He died of congenital heart disease. He was wonderful to us and I was very much in love with him."

Giorgio took this emphatic description for what it was meant to be – proof that Tamara's life had gone on without him.

"Do you have children?" she asked him.

"No," and with the heavy sigh, "we didn't. We were going to, but Celia died so young…" His voice just trailed off.

"I think you would have been a good father," Tamara said. "A very good father."

Giorgio responded with a wan smile.

"Not to be," was all he said.

They worked through their meal with less gusto than they had when once together, but with a growing closeness that was gradually healing the wounds that each felt had been opened again that afternoon. Over the plates of food, the conversation began to come easier, stories on some points were lighter, and both Giorgio and Tamara shed the feeling that they needed to protect themselves or make amends for past events.

At the end of dinner, Giorgio volunteered to walk Tamara back to her hotel, but she demurred. She knew he was just being a gentleman, but she felt that this would be too much like the other string of events, which she wasn't ready to repeat yet.

"What if I told you I worked for the government?" he asked.

Giorgio had run through a brief list of possible biographies and Tamara couldn't tell if he was making up excuses, trying to explain himself without revealing too much, or – now – just playing along with her.

She only shrugged. Putting her hand lightly on his forearm, she responded.

"It doesn't matter, Giorgio. You were married, you were in prison, you worked for the government. Why would I care now? Why should I care?"

He looked down at his broad palms.

"Some things you can't unvolunteer for," was all he could say.

He put her in a cab, told the driver where to take her, and gave the man more than enough money to cover the ride.

"I hope you will let me at least pay for the cab."

"Yes, Giorgio…um, Dante. Yes, of course. Thank you."

As the car pulled away from the curb, Giorgio stood dumbly by, watching the first true love of his life leave again.

Hotel Pistoia, Rome

September 2016

Tamara couldn't sleep at all that night. She had a full-running movie of her short life with Giorgio, both 1985-1986 and now. She wondered what was the point of today's meeting, tonight's dinner. She wondered what destiny had in mind for her.

And with all the thoughts tumbling around in her head, she even wondered why she let Giorgio put her in a cab without giving her his phone number. Unlike 1986, they both had cell phones now, and at about three-thirty in the morning, she was aching to know what his number was.

The comfortable arm chair by the bed was no longer comfortable when she rose from a fitful sleep around seven a.m. Shaking her head to dispel the fog, she looked at the clock, then looked down at her unkempt clothes, yesterday's sweater and jeans that she had been wearing when Giorgio appeared once again in her life.

"What do I do now?" she asked the empty room.

She got up, splashed some water on her face and looked at her blood-shot eyes. Concluding that a shower would not very much improve her appearance, she slipped on some shoes, tied her hair up on top of her head, and went down to the lobby for some breakfast.

As she descended the steps and the lobby came into view, she saw a man's legs slumped forward on a side chair, wearing bright blue Nikes. Tamara quickened her pace as the view increased so that she could see the hands crossed on the lap, then the arms and shoulders, and finally, the gray-speckled tossle of hair on Giorgio's head.

He was sound asleep in the chair. The clerk behind the desk smiled at Tamara as she came into view and nodded in Giorgio's direction.

"*È stato qui dalle sei*," he said. "He's been here since six o'clock."

Tamara walked up Giorgio and placed her fingertips lightly on his shoulder, and he awoke at the touch. But he didn't spring to his feet; he just straightened up slowly, looking closely at Tamara for her reaction – should he stay or should he go?

"Thank you, Giorgio," was all she said.

They both looked terrible, and after a few minutes alone on the sidewalk, they decided to return – she to her room and he to his apartment – and get together later in the morning after a shower and putting on some clean clothes.

Dinner with Julie

March 2017

I could tell that this was all becoming more real for my daughter. Julie's eyes alternately glowed bright and glazed over in concern and doubt. She was worried about me, the memory of her father, and the Italian man she had not met.

"What happened then, mom?"

This long story held my interest but in her unsettled mind, Julie was reaching for the final chapter, wanting to know whether her mother had found another man.

"We went for a long walk. It was just like I remembered it. Giorgio had loosened up a bit – well, I guess I had, too – and we just told stories about our lives."

"Did you tell him about me?" Julie asked anxiously, pouring another glass of wine.

"Of course, I did, honey! That was the best part."

Julie smiled broadly, then I think I detected a slight fade. I didn't want her to think that I had shelved memories of her dad already.

"I told Giorgio everything about our lives together, and how I had had a wonderful twenty-six years with your father. And how you were the rare gem in the center of my life. He smiled warmly at all these stories."

"And what of Giorgio?"

"Well, he was married, as I told you. He had been happy, and he continued his work..."

"As an architect, or...I don't know what to call it."

"Yes, he was an architect. Anyway, we had a very nice day together." I hesitated to say the next thing, but went ahead with my thought.

"It was like old times."

Julie waded through a variety of emotions, but smiled at me and said she was happy for me. She even raised her glass in a toast, and there was an honest gleam in her eye.

Palatine Hill, Rome

September 2016

They sat on the grassy knoll on the Palatine Hill. Tamara listened quietly as Giorgio embarked on one of his history lessons about Rome. By then, she knew much more about the city from her own studies, but she also knew that Giorgio liked to talk about these things.

His words faded into the background of her mind as her thoughts turned to studying him. She wondered why he talked about buildings and walls, concrete things of the past. Despite his warmth, whenever he turned his words to the history of Rome – or Italy generally – he seemed to raise a barrier to more intimate conversation. He sometimes seemed to occupy himself with relics and ruins, instead of the story of his own life.

This was one thing that Tamara noticed was different now. She realized that this habit of switching from the light, breezy conversation about him, his work, and their time together to subjects of history and current events had taken over more of the narrative. She wondered if the gregarious, laughing Giorgio of old had been eroded, and been replaced by a cut-out of the same person. Gregarious and laughing, still, but quieter too, more serious, and less openly introspective.

"Age will do that to you," she said aloud, before realizing that she was giving voice to her own thoughts.

"What's that?" he asked.

A bit embarrassed, she blushed and said, "Nothing. Nothing. Just thinking about life."

The interruption halted his narrative about the Palatine Hill and they sat in silence for a while.

"We have lost so many years," she said. "But we could still have more, and we could have each other."

Giorgio looked at her but didn't know how to respond. He looked off over the hills that framed this part of Rome, across the centuries that were evident in street after street of structures, across time from 1986 to the present.

"Would you allow me to propose to you again?" he asked.

After a pause that seemed both too long and too short, Tamara replied.

"Yes."

Dinner with Julie

March 2017

"Oh, my God, mom! I can't believe this!"

Julie was openly, buoyantly happy with this news. The long, slow narrative about me and the man I loved in Rome had won Julie over. She knew I had been alone and lonely these recent years, and someone who seemed so good, like Giorgio, would be perfect for me.

"When?"

"When what?" I asked.

"Mom...when?? When are you getting married? I can't believe it! I'm so excited!"

Amalfi Ristorante, Rome

September 2016

It took a while for the thought of marriage to seep into Tamara and Giorgio's minds. They had wanted that thirty years earlier, had rediscovered each other again, and had rediscovered the closeness that they felt. As for Giorgio, he found solace in Tamara's presence, and he wanted that very badly.

After a long, unseasonably hot afternoon, they returned each to their own places to shower and dress for dinner. Tamara sat for a while in her hotel room, trying to wrap her mind around all this; Giorgio sat for the same period in his apartment. He had a tall tumbler of red wine at his elbow, a firm but confident look on his face, and an optimism that he had not felt for many years.

Amalfi Ristorante was just around the corner from Tamara's hotel and they agreed to meet there at seven o'clock. She arrived first, gave the head waiter her name, and he immediately grinned at her.

"Ah, signora! Dante is expecting you."

He led her to the table, but there was no one there.

"I thought you said Giorgio – I mean Dante – was waiting."

"Ah, I said Dante is expecting you. But he is not here yet. Please," he continued, "sit down and I'll bring you the bottle of wine he ordered."

Tamara checked her watch and saw that she had arrived ten minutes early.

"Not too anxious, are we?" she asked herself with a smile. Then she remembered that Romans are never on time.

The waiter returned quickly with a bottle of Prosecco and Tamara laughed.

"Of course," she said with a smile.

Ten minutes went by, then twenty. It was now past the seven o'clock reservation but Tamara consoled herself with the thought that no Roman would show up that soon.

"Then again, Giorgio was never late."

Another ten minutes went by and Tamara was starting to worry; cold droplets appeared on the backs of her hands and on the nape of her neck.

The waiter didn't come around for a while, so Tamara went in search of him. The television in the bar area was turned to a news station and the announcer was reading excitedly from a page he held between his two hands.

"*Oggi, c'è stata un'esplosione in un'antica grotta nella parte settentrionale di Roma.*" – "Today, there was an explosion in an ancient cave in the northern part of Rome."

"*Le autorità avevano già concluso che i soldati di ISIS si erano nascosti lì.*" – "The authorities had already concluded that there were ISIS soldiers hiding there."

"*La polizia ha arrestato due uomini ieri, ma non aveva alcuna prova per arrestare gli altri.*" – "The police had arrested two men there yesterday, but had no evidence to arrest the others."

A view of an old mithraeum came on the screen, with its arching portal and angled stones holding up the entrance to the cave. Then the scene switched to the rubble left by the explosion, a horrible scene of rocks and boulders piled up in a dusty heap where the opening once was.

"*Oggi, sono andati. Sepolto nelle macerie.*" – "Today, they are gone. Buried in the rubble."

Tamara returned to the table and, without sitting, gulped down the last of the Prosecco in her glass. Then she pulled her sweater from the back of the chair, wiped away a tear, and stomped toward the door.

Dinner with Julie

March 2017

Stunned into silence, Julie just stared at me. After a long pause, she spoke.

"But he's alive, right?"

I didn't answer, and didn't even look at my daughter. I was struggling once again with the depression and anger that I felt that evening six months before. I couldn't decide whether to love him, hate him, or try in vain to forget him.

"Yes, he's… well, I don't know, actually. I left Italy on a plane the next day. I couldn't stay there any longer. I couldn't go through what I had experienced thirty years ago. So, I left."

I said all that with certainty, a firm conviction, a declaration of my own independence. But that strength deserted me in the next moment, and I broke down crying.

A Country Home, Spain

September 2017

Giorgio sat in a darkened room, absent-mindedly stroking his pencil across a parchment-colored paper. He watched as his hand moved without purpose or direction, spraying lines across the page without obvious beginning or ending. His hands seem to move outside the control of his brain, but he was uninterested in correcting the condition, or forcing his fingers to obey some command that he couldn't formulate.

He stopped the motion after a while and sat still. He looked out the window at the rust-colored leaves of the vineyard beyond his apartment, and let his mind wander.

Then he reached for a clean sheet of paper and began to write, in full control of his hand and his faculties.

"Dear Tamara," he began. "Some things you can't unvolunteer for.

"I am alright, if you have wondered...or even care. I was taken by some people, they were rough and didn't listen to my pleas about you, about finding you. I had performed their task and thought I would be free, but...I wasn't.

"My heart ached that afternoon and evening, and I couldn't tell whether it was just the physical pain of the aging muscle in my chest or the suffering of the soul within it. I missed you for so many years, then I found you. I couldn't lose you again.

"But I am here now. It's a small cottage in the country. Not the country you would think, but, yes, in the country. Though I don't expect you to care. You should be angry. You should hate me. Maybe that would be easiest.

"I wanted to write you this letter to tell you that I love you, then and now. I wanted to write you this letter to comfort you, although I think I surrendered that right when I failed to show up at dinner that evening.

"I was told, that afternoon when we sat on the Palatine Hill...and I knew what I had to do. I was going to help these people, then get away and find you at the restaurant. I wanted to flee before it happened. But they caught me.

"Now, I am once again imprisoned. And I have too few years left to outlive this.

"I will find a way to get this letter to you. It is my confession, it is my plea, neither of which I expect you to acknowledge. I have let you down again.

"I loved Celia, but – Tamara – you were and are the truest love of my life.

"*Amor'è vita,*" Giorgio added at the bottom of the letter – "Love is life."

Just then someone entered his room. The man was unarmed but hovered over Giorgio in an imposing position. He looked down at the letter and lifted it slowly from the desk. Giorgio knew not to protest. The man read through the letter quickly, gave an indifferent shrug, and walked out the door with the piece of paper in his hand.

Dinner Alone

September 2017

Tamara stood looking out the window as the sun fought with gray clouds for dominance of the sky. Streaks of dried tears stained her cheeks.

She lifted her right hand and read the words on the paper once again.

"*Amor'è vita.*"

Lightning Source UK Ltd.
Milton Keynes UK
UKHW041034161120
373486UK00001B/159